"There is no agony like bearing an untold story within you."

Zora Neale Thurston

BELINDA'S LAW

Jerry Bronk

ISBN: 978-1-4669-9627-4 (sc)
ISBN: 978-1-4669-9628-1 (e)

Trafford rev. 08/01/2013

 www.trafford.com

North America & international
toll-free: 1 888 232 4444 (USA & Canada)
fax: 812 355 4082

Chapter 1

"Beginnings are delicate moments, the beginning of a building
no less than the beginning of a friendship or marriage."
Witold Rybcznski

Things were looking up; things were going up. We had the foundation
down; a concrete slab was curing over sand and rebar. Wheelbarrow by
wheelbarrow we mixed the slurry; half-ton by half-ton we hauled water
and the fifty-pound bags of cement. Jake may not have been a jack-of-all-
trades, but he knew enough as both teacher and helper to get my project
going good and down smoothly. The construction was to be mostly an
on-the-job training job. Back then I had a mind full of figuring and
imagining and my hands were busy building. The small house, which
would have, more or less, proceeded according to a sketchy down-on-
paper-plan, was to be mostly a do-it-myself endeavor. I was doing
a pretty good job of keeping to that job, but sometimes my mind did go
back to all the complications and frustrations that I'd left about 400
miles down the road.

The next step would've been laying block, the long walls, to nine feet or
so. I would've preferred working in wood, doing a partial post-and-beam
design, but, while technically in a rain forest we were also in fire-vulnerable
country. There would be no green lawn to separate my outpost from
untamed vegetation. Those walls would've been reinforced to with-stand—
my inexpert opinion—an 8.0 on the Richter. But I didn't worry
about natural disasters. But, I wonder, what if? what if a very
unnatural disaster hadn't struck before we'd even started on those
walls? Not that a project like that is ever finished once-and-for-all.

While taking a break we had contemplated the green hills of as-far-as-
you-could-see second-growth Douglas Fir to the east. Well, "second
growth" was just a guess. Jake knew. That prospect would be the
featured view. I imagined the opposite side with a tomato-red door with,
to emphasize the horizontal profile, a lengthy beam for a lintel.

"Sure gonna be nice," Jake said.
"Sure is," I agreed, well aware that Jake lived in a single-room, flea-bag
hotel. Well, not literally lousy; I knew because I had stayed there. From
the third floor of that hotel I could see the crescent-shaped harbor. That
was maybe a quarter century after the event, but here and there it still
showed where the man-made had been attacked by a series of waves. Fishing boats
had been tossed into harbor-side buildings and some well into town. Old-
timers had told me that some kids up from Humboldt State were leery of
an acount of a deadly tidal wave. People killed? By some oceanic oddity
an earthquake in Alaska had fatal repercussions in California. The
number of dead was a bit different with each telling but a dozen was a
good guess.

"I had a nice house once," Jake informed.

"The missus get it?" I guessed.

"Ya, well, they generally do you know. Course if I hadn't been drinkin' it mighta been a different story."

"Shit happens." I didn't know if there had been a children situation and I didn't want to know, not that they'd be kids now. Ya, kids. I'd gone up there to put down some literal stakes; that was after pulling up some emotional ones: the high stakes kind that some men kill over.

I took a swig from the wet-burlap covered water bottle and picked up the spade. Plumbing wouldn't be a reality for a while and an outhouse would make things more homey and civilized. The house-to-be was more than a cabin or a hippie A-frame; it was not a cheap-as-possible shelter. When I was a kid I saw a photo-feature of a beautifully simple and unique house. I remembered that two lengths of stone walls supported beams; the rock ramparts extended past the width of the building and protected the glass walls which were the other sides of a rectangle. The design was both rugged and elegant. So, decades after my first architectural interest, I was to build, with that general design in mind, albeit block instead of rock— with what some pay to remodel a kitchen—an abode both modest and ambitious, some-what original and some of it derivative.

Finished for the day, I would drive Jake into Crescent City and get some dinner and a thermos of coffee at Jean's diner. We'd stowed in the pickup along side my sleeping bag, the chain saw, sledge, trowels and assorted tools when Jake asked, "See that car?" From our plateau we could see a vehicle raising a haze of dust on the old logging road.

"That's a sheriff's car." My handy man had an eagle eye.

"You can tell from here?"

"Believe me," Jake emphasized, "I know a Del *Nort* County sheriff's car when I see one." He rolled down each sleeve of his plaid shirt and buttoned up.

I hadn't anticipated any law-enforcement activity. We were miles from the Klamath River tensions and the possibility of a cross-fire between, maybe Greens, fishermen, lumbermen, marijuana growers, sweet-potato farmers, Indians, feds, survivalists and who could be allied with who-knows, local law enforcement. Not with any of that line-up in mind, however, I thought it would be a good idea to keep an eye out for a used 12-gauge.

It had been another lifetime since I'd been an on-the-road hitch-hiker, but the sight of a roof-rack of cop-lights gave me a stab of apprehension. The tan, dusty and side-starred Ford four-door slowed to turn off the road and bounced on to the barely passable not-yet-a-driveway. After hesitating a moment to check a clipboard, a uniformed and side-armed deputy got out. "Oh, shit," I told Jake. I had a feeling this wasn't about septic-tank plans or off-the-grid concerns. To disarm myself I leaned the spade up against the truck; to meet the brown-skinned, tan-clad lawman half-way, I walked down our barely-trod path.

He told me, "You Jeffrey W Hodges?"

Chapter 2

"A system grinder hates the truth."
Ralph Waldo Emerson

"I've been here twenty years, I've handled hundreds of cases and
only one guy was innocent," said Mrs Conseco. She was an Investigative
Probation Officer. I didn't know such an office existed. That was one of
many mandatory appearances at various venues. Despite that axiomatic
premise as a starting point, those sessions—four? maybe more, all those
doings are pretty blurry—were productive. They were much different
than those court appearances where I couldn't say much. Back then, with
Mrs Conseco I could state my opinion and attempt a presentation
contrary to not only accusations but a very strange "profile." Rita was
her primary informant. She was writing the officer imagined and lengthy
descriptions of not just crimes, not just my pathetic parenting skills, but a
whole damn biography. It seemed that to augment accusations my background had to be built to support a dreadful determinism. My noncriminal
and fairly conventional "persona" had, according to Rita, been
"constructed" to deceive: just her or was it an all-and-everybody
plan? I don't know.

Mrs Conseco adjusted her bifocals, consulted a folder—*my* folder?—
and asked, "You were an altar-boy?" Was she remembering some very
ancient movie? But that had Rita's prints on it; altar-boy meant victim,
victim meant molester.

"Yes, I was for a short while and no I wasn't thank you."
"Rita contends that you and your siblings were molested by your father,
is that so?"

I learned later that to be such a victim, when the defendant doesn't have a
leg to stand on, is an advisable tactic. I don't imagine, however, that Rita
was volunteering that story as a mitigating circumstance. I rolled my eyes
and leaned forward to emphasize the absurdity of that finding and asked,
"Isn't this fiction becoming clearer?"
"Just answer the question."
"Certainly not, but to some experts that's just a 'failure to remember.'"
"A failure to remember, yes, I get that a lot."
"Your sister," she returned to her documentation and said, "is a prostitute,
is that true?"
"Was," I smiled sourly, "call-girl I think you would've called her."
"Most prostitutes were molest or rape victims."
"I guess that's the case." I leaned back, not in resignation but to indicate
my detachment from that line of inquiry. "Who ever is doing this research,
they're decades behind the times. That information and probably most of
that odd history is more than ancient."

*Who was getting that old stuff? Did Rita know about the time me
and Les Johnson broke into . . . ?"*

"I guess she meant she was."

"Karen wasn't any victim; she was on top of the game; she drove her
Mustang with the top down."

"Oh, really. Do you have contact with her?"

"She's in Santa Monica. We phone now and then." I didn't mention that
I'd just received a very helpful check from Karen; A "loan" that we both
knew wasn't. It may have been, to account for her generosity, from a gold card account.

We sat in a cubicle, crowded with file cabinets. Framed photos of a
young man and woman, probably college-age, seemed angled to keep an
eye on the uncomfortable defendant sitting on the well-worn
uncomfortable folding chair. What, I'd sometimes wondered, was the
function of the photo display at one's work place? But, without thinking,
I was thinking of a man's desk. Do woman use images of their spouse and
offspring differently than men? Perhaps they are more of a connection
and a comfort and less as symbol and talisman: or, perhaps not.

At that range I could read the officer's eyes and she, undoubtedly skilled
at such could probably discern what I was feeling. I wasn't too nervous
or sociopathically calm. I was, I hoped, just the concerned citizen. Did
she, like the right-half-the-time polygraph, read involuntary reactions as
tells? indications of lies, half-lies or even veracity?

"Rita, as a good feminist, ought to be admiring of her; she's autonomous
and making do with her assets; she's in charge, she did charge and now
she's getting along quite nicely."

"Rita seems to have a different take."

I thought it both ominous and interesting that Rita had, on my family, any "take" at all. The case had nothing to do with them. I was the accused, the central figure, the axiomatically guilty. Later I learned that, paradoxically, it was unsolicited information from *her* family that, if it didn't save my ass it did mitigate the whipping that I got.

"Rita states that you were somewhat of a bum, almost a hobo. Also you were a compulsive seducer."
Oh, god, except for the "compulsive," would that that were true.
"That's simply not true." Even back then I thought that last characterization sort of an anachronism. Seducer! I don't think I've ever, certainly not in the sense that I think she meant it . . .

"Why would she say those things?"
Why! "Why, I think it's obvious why. I also think it's blatantly obvious that her descriptions are so inaccurate as to be pathetically comical."
"She knew you for . . . how many years."
"Well," I said with too much enthusiasm, "Rita doesn't seem to know the difference between . . . and, ya, she knew me long enough to know . . . that I wasn't—can you imagine?—a hobo."

The officer just looked at me calmly, confidently and in charge. Her stern and implacable expression, extending up from her no-nonsense blue suit, said that she was the judge here.

"Doesn't this muck-raking," I asked stupidly with weary resignation, "tell us more about the raker than the supposed mucker?"

Mrs Conseco wrapped up our interview, squared away her papers as if to indicate that this case was just a matter of routine processing, and sent me away with a slight smile. A knowing smile? a sardonic smile? or just a tic of customer relations?

Chapter 3

"The source of one's joy is often the source of one's sorrows."
Jessamyn West

Even if you've never been married, you still have parental rights,"
she advised. I'd had, previous to the more serious phase, not a criminal
lawyer but a family lawyer. Yes, I thought, especially when you've been
doing the week-end baby-sitting and kicking in support. The latter was only fair and I
really looked forward to minding our kid.

"It's been almost a year, an agonizing year, since I've seen my daughter."
Ms Harlinger maintained her professionally concerned and objective
bearing which seemed to call for "just the facts" and no over-emoting.

"Let me read you a transcript I made of some telephone conversations,"
I offered. "Not that this is verbatim, but . . . ."
"You took notes, why?"
"A friend said this woman sounds dangerous, he said I should take notes

on calls that could be evidence, maybe incriminating evidence." I'd typed up, from my scribbled notes for any interested parties, about twenty double-spaced pages.

"OK, let's hear it." Her long-looped silver ear rings swayed from young and innocent ears. What dangerous and disturbing accounts had those ears heard from the stressed, the angry, the injured, the vengeful, the drugged and maybe even some possessed?

I read: "September 20th, '88. Rita calls, she's in a state again. I can hear Belinda crying. I try to calm Rita. She responds, 'You're not going to calm me down. You're the one that screwed this up from the beginning.'"
Screwed this up from the beginning?
"What did she mean by that?" I ask rhetorically. Does my lawyer catch the seeming double-meaning in that assertion or am I being too literal?
"Rita goes on about her health, I won't go into detail, and her stress and this is all my fault because of my 'peer' relationship with Bel. 'Just don't call here again'—she called that time, but I call more often—'Bel can call you if she is good, *really* good, but don't you call. Goodbye.'"

"You get the picture?" She grimaces and nods, her silver waves aside her strikingly pale-peach complexion. *How long has she been in practice?*
I continue, "Bel calls, she's crying, it takes a minute before she can talk. I ask if she's been acting bad. 'I'm sorry daddy, yes, I'm sorry, I'm so . . .' She says mama won't let her play soccer tomorrow. I tell her I don't think that is a good punishment, but—what can I say?—soccer just isn't as important as our troubles, which is pathetically beside-the-point."

I explain to Ms Harlinger, while her chic-short black hair crowns an expression that nods in seeming sympathetic comprehension, that it goes on-and-on like this: my desperate and clumsy long-distance attempts to reconcile Bel with her mother, myself with her mother and Belinda's heart-rending attempts to . . . what? not live in fear? to see her dad? to make things the way they were?

"She says she heard a click," I was reading again. "I say I didn't hear it, but I did. I emphasize the 'be good/you can call' connection. She seems to be feeling better now, certainly the crying, the painful, wracking sobs have subsided. I tell her, 'I love you very much and always will no matter what.'"

"OK," Harlinger said as if she got the point, "let me make copies of what you have."
Well, all that—and more—got a "family counselor" procedure going.

"Daddy," she ran across the parking lot and—as she had always done —jumped into my arms. She had grown, just as kids always do.
The heft of her was unfamiliar. Her baby-blond hair was turning to the prosaic dun of her parents.

"It's so so so good to see you again."
She smiled with both unease and enthusiasm. The easy conversation that had been an unbreakable bond, was now awkward. I said the obvious.
Bel responded, "I'm the second tallest kid in my class."
I didn't know how to credit such an achievement. "I'll bet you're one of the smartest in the second grade, too." She grinned an acknowledgment.

Rita approached. She had grown too, but not upwards. I took the initiative and said, "Hello, Rita." She managed an appropriate response with even a slight smile. "Thanks for coming," meaning thanks for some neutral expert to disabuse her of the fixed idea that I was an inappropriate and inept parent and that I could, again, be a daddy to our daughter. I, of course, was paying.

"Well," she said, "maybe we can straighten some things out." "Things," of course, had nothing to do with her. She held out her hand to Bel; Bel let go of my hand and took the other: the obvious upper hand.

The proceedings, a half-dozen or so, were a tribunal: three against one. Dr Dietz, seemingly oblivious of any malevolence, sided with the aggressor; the aggressor positioned herself between Belinda and me. She kept her close, Belinda acceded. Finally, in exasperation and realization, I asked, "You're not accusing me of sexual abuse, are you?" "Oh, no, of course not."

Later I thought that response a little too ready, a little too emphatic. I didn't know it then, but those words may have been the last words— face-to-face words—that she spoke to me. There were, as I remember, more hysterical phone-call accusations. And then, during various proceedings, she, so very cool and collected, would talk about me but not to me.

"Did you dance with her?" the Dr asked me, not accusingly, but . . . just to ask . . . !
"Yes, we danced. Bel got a big kick out of it."
"Belinda, what sort of dancing did you do?" the expert asked. His blue

and yellow polka-dot bow-tie seemed to signify that what goes on above
here is superficial and devoid of insight.

Belinda answered in a flat, reluctant voice, "Sorta rock 'n roll, I guess."
Where did that dancing issue come from? Rita and I went dancing at
Eli's once. It was, well, disappointing; we were rhythmically at odds.
Which was odd because sexually we were more than compatible; we
were in accord in more than only that arena, but things changed; they
changed when she became pregnant; they changed when Bel was born;
in fact from that day they'd kept changing until there was nothing
between us except Bel. Then Bel came between us because Rita seemed
to think there was a custody battle going on: *who would take possession?*
I wasn't competing, I wasn't stirring conflict; I was, for all of our sakes,
trying to accommodate, trying to keep the lid on.

It's long ago, long ago before we converged at Dr Dietz' office, but
we once had, I thought, a mutually advantageous its-all-about-sex
relationship. Now I was accused of having "dates" with Belinda.
Something was always handy for me to be guilty of. I didn't stay long
enough when I dropped Bel off. Then I stayed too long. Major
disapproval when Bel was delivered with evidence indicating that there
had been no bath over the week-end.

She had perfected the sigh of exasperation; a resigned exhalation that she
used like a cutting tool. She would unsheathe that all-purpose implement
at any act—or lack of—that she thought was thoughtless, careless or
just oblivious. She seemed to be trying for a good belt to the chops; was
that intentional or just her reflexive antagonism? Did she have a motive
for this "get-daddy-mad" provocation? I wouldn't ever accommodate
such asked-for-it unpleasantness. No, certainly not.

15

As the tribunal wore on, Bel became more and more distant: distant from me and distant from herself: No spark to her blue eyes, less animation, her demeanor sullen. That progressive dissociation sickened me. Rita sat, her arm around Bel, smug, satisfied, a soul killer. Possession, it seemed, was more than nine tenths of it. I didn't know it then, but that despairing meeting was the last time I would see our daughter.

I tried to do that—to see Bel—for six months or so. That meant ongoing lawyer and counseling fees. And a lot of driving. I imagined when that did happen, Bel would, as she had always done until our last meetings, jump into my arms with an enthusiastic "Daddy." But, to be realistic: no, she was changing as kids do, but she was also adopting a persona both inauthentic and necessary. The reality was that the optimistic scenario was not to be. I gave up.

I had, for the last seven or eight years been picking up and delivering drugs and medical supplies to clinics and nursing homes for MEDelivery. Five different routes and the traffic on each was getting more than frustrating. After I sold my Mazda hatch-back and got a good deal on a not too used pickup (both lucky, a friend needed a car, a guy needed cash), I told Fred when I came into work that in two weeks he'd have to do without me. I would give up my main campaign (and the incidental job) and start a new project. The Lost Coast beckoned (fishing was down, lumber was down, real estate was, I guessed, not going up).

To do that, however, meant getting rid of. stuff, all those acquisitions. Stuff that becomes almost a part of us, the TV for instance. That dependable but much-derided appliance brought me the Raiders, the

Warriors, the Giants and other war-like entities; and sometimes
occasional actual wars and other fascinating if not entertaining
catastrophes. And an occasional laugh. And "Sesame Street," but that
wasn't quite the same without Bel.

Seth, a quite human companion, came over and relieved me of some of
the accumulation. An old boom-box would do for his garage while he
tended to his on-going project of rebuilding an Alfa Romeo Spyder that
was well past its days of the sporting life. Perhaps his Bill Evans, Davis
and Art Tatum tapes would keep his work at a measured and inspired
pace. *Potted plants,* yet, and books: who would appreciate them?
Seth's kids were too old for Bel's books. Her fancy thrift-shop sweaters,
her Barbies, her model horses and a lot of good stuff went to Goodwill.
Much that was easier to part with went into somebody's dumpster.

I'd forgotten about some of the books. Others, like "The Velveteen
Rabbit," I remembered had been dramatically presented by Cathy. We
still had two L Frank Baum volumes had come from Judy's collection.
I hadn't been in touch; should I call and give them back to her? I
remember Bel's wide eyed expression when—at four, or was it five?—
we opened the package from my mother that contained old and very
used Beatrix Potter and *Pooh* books. She looked at one and then
another and another and then looked up at me with an expression of
wonder over what she knew was a treasure better than any old new book.

Chapter 4

*"Somehow it feels the world is having more effect on me
than I'm having on the world."*
Ashley Brilliant

"What ever happened to Cathy?" Seth asked.

"I don't know, she split, we split—not that we'd had that much to split.
She wasn't a goin' steady type of gal . . . jeez, that was a long ago, what
ever . . . ?" I didn't want to contemplate the image that came to mind: just
one of many memories of Cathy, but still . . . . "Look," she'd exclaimed as
if really pissed, "look, what you've done to me." "Oh, well, a little welt,"
I'd responded much too casually, as if I was proud of making my mark,
"it won't show." "Show!" who knows what kind of role I'll be
auditioning for?" She gave her bath towel a decisive wrap and
tucked it in over her breasts and pivoted into the bathroom. Seth
watched the ash grow on his cigar and commented, "She sure was . . . ."
"She sure was," I concurred thinking of those breasts, her skin so sheer
they revealed a faint trace of blue vein.

I just continued puffing the comforting smoke of a Honduran cigar and put my feet up on the redwood coffee table where I had habitually parked them; my construction was doing duty on Seth's smoking porch. Back then I was facing the real possibility of a much less comfortable environment. A world of dangerous company, no cigars, no beer to wash down worse-than-army chow, and continuous and ominous noise. I'd looked forward to getting out of that army where, at least, you got paid. In prison you paid—one way or another. Especially one in my lowly status.

"So, after jabbing you, knocking you around when you're defenseless, this bitch—I can refer to her as a "bitch?"

"Sure, sounds right to me."

"This bitch goes for the knock-out."

"Tit for tat, I knocked her up, she knocks me down." That—had my sense of humor been knocked askew?—was so funny that I damn near snuffed Seth's good stuff out my nose. Ya, I thought, I should have seen it coming, but still, *she didn't play by the rules.*

"Frankly, the few times I saw them together, I thought *that poor kid.*"

"You can't choose your parents, but apparently that's what Bel has done."

I'd come over to Seth's and Irene's, just as I'd done before my move north. Now, besides some congenial companionship and a change from my pick-up-as-residence, they supplied me with water. I, like some droughted-out refugee, arrived with various plastic bottles. Another critical bottle was the one I pissed in. I dumped that waste down a storm drain which is probably illegal but better than looking for a rest room —or getting caught, red-faced and red-handed committing public urination. That was just one of the trying contortions of living in a truck, but I was lucky that I still didn't have that hatch-back.

"If there was any justice, you'd be getting custody."

Custody . . . ? with roles reversed: did I want that? Did I ever want that? Well, I'd want that only . . . *only?* as a means of saving Bel from her mother's cold and over-wrought so-called parenting. I never really wanted the the *job* of having a kid, the real responsibility. I just had our delightful child for week-ends: for entertaining and affectionate interludes which was fine for all concerned. Or, so it seemed. Well, not exactly "fine." The arrangement was always tenuous; the hierarchical relationship was always fragile at the top; at the bottom I appreciated what is a common emotion, but seems a singular kind of love. But I skated on thin ice. And then, when the legal and therapy burdens were piling up, I was worse than broke. Even when working I was making considerably less than Rita the high-school teacher.

"The custody to worry about is the kind they take you into," I said. Seth stubbed out his cigar and commented, "Jeff, you sure got your ass in a bind". We sat in silence at that truism and let the evening fade to dark.

"What've you got . . . a month before . . . ?"

"Ya, about that."

"OK, we'll take a victory lap then, a 'stay-out-of-jail' free ride."

"No shit, you'll have it running?"

Seth indulged in a few self-satisfied nods of confidence, and he rapped his knuckles on the table top for emphasis; or was that an unconscious knock on wood?

"You can help me sand it down for a paint job."

Irene made an appearance and poured herself a drink in Seth's glass. She rested her head on his shoulder. Her flowing chestnut hair with

some "I-don't-care-gray" spilled over Seth's sweat shirt . . . A good woman
to stand by you, to lie by you, that was so . . . nice. "Jeff, isn't there something,
a letter to the judge, something that says your a good guy and . . . ?
"That's thoughtful, Irene, but I figure I could only ask four people and
that just wouldn't look all that impressive."
"Jeez," Seth said, "that's sorta depressing."

I did a comic recoil. "I didn't think of it in quite that way, but, gee,
thanks, maybe now . . . ." I'd felt as if I was drifting, drifting farther and
farther away from my more-or-less normal life; a life with intervals of
love and some secure friendships. There was the agonizing, drawn-out
loss of Belinda, but now my primary concern had, either by common
sense or a kind of survival instinct, had changed from her to myself.
Now, however, the self of me was all adrift and all connections were
vulnerable and any new such improbable. That feeling, which became
dominant, would change me from a "loner" who could afford to think
that everybody else was out of step to just a lonely guy who had to
watch his step.

We sat with a homey light coming through the windows at our back.
Seth poured us another couple of fingers of his smooth and mellow
drink. Irene continued, "Well, if . . . if you change your mind, I've got a
pretty good idea of what to write."

I didn't want to talk about the case, I didn't want to refer to the
seriousness of the accusations which—mainly because of Flynn—
the charges, or the charge that we pled to a deal on were much less
threatening, much less so because the accusations were more than

suspect, but, as such things work, a compromise still means a penalty. What that charge was I didn't know—it was all fiction.

"Maybe we should've sent a letter without asking you; you told us who the judge was," Seth said.
I wouldn't have objected to that; actually I would've appreciated it— when I found out about it. I took another tack and said, "The probation officer told me something unexpected. Seems that her sisters and a friend wrote Mrs Conseco to the effect that they didn't know much about me, but they were very suspicious about Rita."

Seth, with a thoughtful grimace, pinched his chin. Irene, as if to express a high degree of dubiosity, pulled at her lower lip with a forefinger. I eyed the water jugs and they seemed to trigger the memory of bucketing water out of the Smith River to mix with the cement. That had been a promising time, a time after a great loss but here I was again in the loss column.

"Jeff," she said out of the blue, "you should've stuck with . . . . the one before Rita, the blond."

Well, yes, sure, considering the subsequent history, but "stuck" isn't quite the word to use concerning that very mobile and fancy-free creature.

Chapter 5

"I hear much of people's calling out to punish the guilty, but very few are concerned to clear the innocent."
Daniel Defoe

Mrs Conseco settled in her lumbar support office chair. She seemed, after several visits, less the "I've-seen-it-all" judge. The gray-walled cubicle was less of a threat of confinement. The brown-eyed brother and sister still looked on from their perch, but I ignored them. I acknowledged the officer and sat on the worn-to-a-shine folding chair. She opened "my" case book and skimmed several of the surprisingly many pages. Then she sat back, as if to do her job from a relaxed posture, ran an ample forefinger down her cheek to touch a gold necklace and asked, "What were you doing way up in Crescent City?

"I was building a house, a ways south of there, inland."

"That's interesting. You've worked construction?"

"No, never did." I could have said that I've worked more than a few jobs, but that info was not just beside-the-point, but of negative value considering . . . .

She frowned in feigned confusion. "But you know how to build . . . ?"

"Not exactly, it was an OJT project."

She smiled as if amused and went back to her folder of who-knows-what-all. "You know, I don't remember a case, well a minor case like yours, that involved so much correspondence?" she said if this was not a burden, but to use her word "interesting." I'd contributed only a few pages, a brief my side-of-the-story. Rita had burdened Mrs Conseco with the equivalent of a novella. I wasn't privy to any of it except that which the investigator chose to allude to.

"Rita says you have over $60,000 in CDs."

"I never discussed never even mentioned any money situation with her. I don't know how she'd know that I had any money except that I paid—paid more than my share."

"That's not what she says."

"Well, whose share is what isn't that easy to determine, but she never said anything about it, never complained."

She, as if in deep thought mode, scrunched her face and tapped her upper lip lightly with three fingers. "I got a call from her sister . . . in San Diego. We talked for, oh, a good half-hour."

"And?"

"What she had to say was pretty interesting." She thought some more and then went to her papers. "Did you know anything about Rita and her grandfather?"

Now I scrunched. "No."

"Did you know that her father, for that and other reasons, cut her out of his will, disinherited her?"

Wow, that took me by surprise. What was "that" and "other reasons"? I had
to restrain myself, but I asked, "and reasons"?

"Money stuff."

"And in that correspondence, Rita was asking for . . . for how much?"

"A lot." She consulted the text again. "So how does a delivery truck driver
happen to have $60,00?"

"I had maybe half that; her monetary imagination seems . . . seems quite
ambitious." A good part of that was in the grip of a real estate agent who had
informed me that because of my "improvements" I would be taking a loss
on that deal.

"So you were delivering drugs?" She had come back to my so mysterious
money.

"Yes, I was and both pick up and delivery are pretty secure procedures."
The combination of money and drugs certainly arouses a cop's suspicion;
and I was a sitting duck. I suppose someone with both the skill and the
inclination could profit from such access, but I certainly had neither. The
officer just mmm'd at my statement and, taking another line of inquiry,
said, "You've traveled quite a bit."

"Not that much, not for quite a while."

"Have you been to Thailand?"

I gave her a "what-the-hell-are-you-getting-at" look.

"I've had cases with that . . . ah, connection. Mexico?"

"Sure, who hasn't?

I could have, to satisfy her curiosity, volunteered that I had failed to check
the ID of a young hooker in Tangier. That assignation in the Medina was
memorable for being so nicely ominous. Directed by Hassan, Hussein, one
of those aitchy names, who, as best I remember was a red-headed Berber

from the Rif country and an all-purpose dealer and opportunist, I went several maze-like turns past the three-table restaurant where I went for cous-cous. Then I climbed three flights of dim-lit and pungent stairs and as promised, was the somewhat alluring object of my need. Such reminiscences—not that any tales of that sort would be told—would only confirm the squalid character-study proffered to the prosecution by Rita.

"I had another conversation." She paused and grimaced. "I called Rita; I talked with Belinda." She tapped her pen to her jaw as if considering. "She said you raped her . . . multiple times."

Another sickening blow. It shouldn't have come as a surprise. After all, as far as I knew, Bel had told a consistent story to cops in Berkeley and Modesto and to who knows how many therapists. And to her mother; or was it vice versa? Later Dr Maye would elicit from one of those therapists that Bel had divulged—with how much prompting?—that "I might have been molested when I was small." He also learned that Belinda's claim was very nearly the same as an account told to Rita by a friend of hers. The guy was on the ball. I wasn't . . . on the ball. Such distortions of reality were disorienting. My head was a muddle of desperate emotions that conflicted with ominous facts: facts both true and false. The truth was just a pitiful beside-the-point plea. I was laid low. Perhaps it was just as well that I wasn't working.

"Hey, Fred, I have to take tomorrow afternoon off."
"Damn, that puts me in a bind. What for?"
"Well, there is a court hearing that I have to be at."
"What the hell do you have to do with court?"
"Well, you see . . . ah . . . ."

Fortunately that conversation never happened. Fortunately I wasn't working. Not collecting unemployment-not-working: just not working. My attendance was required at various functions, but other than those I was free. I wasn't supposed to go out of state, or maybe it was the county, I forget. The down-side was that in addition to living expenses I was paying two lawyers, an on-going family court counseling/investigation operation, plus Bel's previous therapy—the theater where the accusations were probably elicited—and a child support payment. Then later, which displaced some of those, I was sentenced-to every week psychotherapy. Luckily I had my pickup with a camper shell. Another lucky possession was an old wind-up shaver. I could hardly count my blessings.

The next and last time I saw Mrs Conseco, I asked, "rape, multiple," were those Belinda's words?"

"That's essentially what she said. She was very distraught. I told her I was sorry for having to ask her about this again."

"Thank you."

"For?"

"For telling her you were sorry." I couldn't imagine the metamorphosis that Bel was enduring. We were both in pain, but certainly her suffering was the greater and of greater consequence: it would be with her the rest of her life, her much longer life.

We just sat there for a moment, then she looked down at the piling up of my case. Then she raised her head and said, "The usual is a year in Santa Rita."

"I'm not going to any lock-up."

"Well, Mr Hodges, that's hardly up to you."

"There's one thing I have control over."

She paused a beat, than stuck out her hand and said, "Good luck."

"Thank you." We shook hands.

Chapter 6

"Law is . . . whatever is boldly asserted and plausibly maintained."
Aaron Burr

It doesn't matter what you did or didn't do; it's what kind of case the DA can build."
Such a reality check from an ex-DA was not encouraging. Thousands up front and more
to cough up and I start, as I'm sure all defendants do: in a vulnerable and an under-dog
position.

I'd given Flynn—the referral from lawyer Harlinger—a rather emotional run-down of
the factors leading to that surprise attack. He interrupted, "It doesn't matter if the mother
is a bitch; it's the child making accusations". I'd put the transcripts of those telephone
conversations on his desk. He shoved them back without a glance. "Irrelevant." A nine-
year old is, in a legal interpretation, a responsible and independent and agent and any
influence of the mother is irrelevant. I was stuck with this lawyer and this other, legal
reality.

"Trial?"

"First of all you wouldn't make a very good witness." That was encouraging. Meaning

what? I didn't look right? I didn't talk right? I couldn't play the role of the wronged
defendant?

"The jury wouldn't like you."

Oh, dear, I thought, what will I do for self-esteem after this guy shows me that he's the
man in charge? His office was big; he sat in a big chair behind a big desk. Photos and
documents on the big wall certified that he was a big man. He did, I will say, get me out
on OR at our first hearing. A hearing where a cop a few chairs away sneered. I turned and
gave him a "if-looks-could-kill" stare. The only custody I'd been in was a few minutes in
the Del Norte Sheriff's office. I'd been incommunicado—out there off that old logging
road—and that office was just delivering a message from the Berkeley PD: I was to get
my ass down there. I called the cops and they said they'd like to talk to me. I called, from
more than a year ago, lawyer Harlinger: she referred Flynn. He, of course, assumed he
had another guilty client. He explained how cops can get you to say things that you
wouldn't want to say; you don't want to talk to the cops. But, I wonder, what if?

When I was in Flynn's waiting room a crest-fallen young fellow exited the office. He was
deflated, stunned, his eyes revealed no sense of self-possession. I was in minor shock and
not thinking too well, but I never let my head down. None of that line-up of officials,
adversarial or otherwise was going to diminish me.

So, it was with Flynn that I made a series of appearances, hearings, whatever all those
tedious and ominous proceedings were. And speaking of tedious there were the numerous
calls that were sometimes returned, some times not. This was before cell phones and any
return calls went to a very prevailed-upon Seth's answering machine. The phrase "my
lawyer" is humorously misleading. You don't have a lawyer as much as the lawyer has
you; each client has a sometime accessible slice of a much-divided attention.

All the strategizing and analyzing that we—well, he more than me—led to the finale: the sentencing. In attendance were a dozen or so "nolo" or "pleaded guilty" defendants; some were segregated up front—"in the dock," I guess—in orange jump-suits. Others, like me, were plain-clothed and, more or less just a part of the packed court room. We were all "plea" people; nobody was there for a trial. I waited for it seemed an uncalled for long time for the judge's not exactly-down-in-black-and-white judgment. It was not a certainty that the deal was good and I would walk out convicted, but I would "walk." Is that correct con-talk, or does one have to be judged "not guilty" to "walk?"

"You don't seem to understand, Mr Hodges, this isn't exactly an objective inquiry; this is about nailing your balls to the wall." That was yet another lawyer. Along with the criminal case were the Stanislaus County family court proceedings. Some of these were judicial where, for some reason, I was muzzled to a "yes" or a "no," while Rita had ample opportunity to express her reality. A reality that she believed to be true? a reality that *had* to be true? or a reality that was true because it seemed so credible? I don't know, not then, not now.

Other meetings involved county therapists who were supposed to do conflict resolution and be truth-finders. "Mr Hodges, why do you keep lying to us?" asked a Dr Morales, a well-dressed—summer-tan suit, cool blue shirt—little man who was the senior of two "counselors," investigators, what ever they were. He was an interesting, almost entertaining fellow. His guiding principle was "children don't lie." That then-current dogma was probably an over-reaction to the wrongfully held position that children's accusations are, generally, fantasies and not to be taken too seriously. He, I guess, thought himself an enlightened advocate for a valid reality, but his know-it-all, moralizing and simplistic inquiry was . . . inquisitorial. If I was charged with a crime, well, what could I be but guilty? I had to explain to the PhD that a "nolo" plea, although it always resulted in a "guilty" verdict, wasn't an admission of guilt; it wasn't to be referred to as a "guilty" plea.

If he as the "bad" cop, Ms Linz, who I'm sure was as moral as Morales, was the "good" cop. Her primary concern was Belinda's welfare. She even took an interest in those telephone transcripts that I introduced. Rita interjected and pointed out that Bel's tantrums happened when she returned from a week-end with me; this-then-that was obvious evidence. The dowdily dressed Ms Linz seemed to concede that inquiry to the PhD's silk tie and Rita's tidily-dressed reasoning. We were in a small room. I could've taken two steps, grabbed a fist-full of Rita's shoulder-length hair and broke her neck across the back of her chair. I cringed to suppress a smile for indulging in such pointless fantasy. I looked each speaker in the eye; Rita, never addressing me but always talking about me, never met my eye. But she was the cool. under control and well-informed informant. "I've tried to reason with him for years; I knew something was wrong—he just doesn't know how to relate to children—and I was wrong not to know just how much he intimidated her." She had the scenario down. Such rationale was standard then—true or false, either way, it usually made the case.

"They're sending men and some women to what amounts to life on the testimony of kids who say they were raped in outer space," Lawyer Argenio explained after I fumed after one of those sessions. "The accusations against you are banal, the usual; they are, for family court, just a standard "bad dad" case."

That family court "investigation" started with the "facts" of the accusation and, as far as I can remember, never gave any indication that what I was accused of may never have happened. Did, for instance, that court ever have access to the information that Mrs Conseco acquired? Including, especially, the many pages that Rita supplied which, I suspect, favored me the more that corpus expanded. It was a very confusing time and I don't think either Flynn or Argenio wanted to be bothered too much by my opinions and observations. That family fiasco ended, however, when I was sentenced at Superior Court; at Court number four at the Alameda County Court House; that handsome white marble building that stands alone, as if a symbol of justice, on its green lawn against the blue back-drop of Lake Merritt.

Chapter 7

*"The fundamental fault of the female character is that it
has no sense of justice."*
Shopenhauer

I was sentenced to, among other things, therapy. Which, as many of
us know, be it voluntary, advised or very mandatory, is quite expensive.
We didn't get off to a good start, Dr Maye and me. He probably
assumed just another criminal client with a depressingly banal and
excessively subjective history: Understandable.

In response to his dismissive demeanor, I said, "Look, there is no reason
for you to believe me, but just for the record, I didn't do what I've been
accused of, or for that matter, anything criminal."
"You've been convicted," he responded with resignation, "you're a
criminal."
"You've got that half right, that's a start."

The Doctor leaned back in his chair, crossed his arms across his X-large chest and sized-up the patient. He had the size on me if it should come to a physical show-down. The improbable, my imagination had learned, was perversely possible. But I sat calmly as if unconcerned. The worst had happened.

The Dr seemed . . . what? concerned? irritated? That opening was probably new to him. But it was more a defense than a gambit.
"You were found guilty; in fact you pleaded guilty."
"I pled nolo, *no contest,* and that against the advice of two lawyers to 'give them something.' I admitted no guilt which I'm told doing so and staying out of some imprisonment is a rarity."

"How's your daughter doing?"
How is my daughter doing?

"She's obviously, for years . . . had to endure more than she could bear."
I let my self-righteousness seethe and my long drawn-out exhale was almost a whistle through clenched lips. "But, well . . . I don't know what was going on with those three or more therapists, but I'd guess that Belinda's welfare was not their first priority."
"That's a pretty unequivocal statement to make."
"I think it'll become clear as we go along. Let's just say . . . about the process that resulted in accusations against me, about which I know almost nothing, well . . . we can only speculate for now . . . maybe forever."
"You know you just contradicted yourself."
OK, I thought, the Dr wants precision. *I can be precise.*

After a half-dozen sessions, after we had some background and the gist
of the case out of the way, we tended to two different subjects. One
was the post-sentencing, post-county proceedings situation, ie, the
attempt to see Belinda, which would require an OK from her therapist,
a judge, from Rita, and most critically, from Belinda. The process,
which involved my going to Modesto to talk with her therapist several
times, never made any progress. *What if she recanted?* It was then, more
than three years since I'd seen her, I gave up and drove up to Crescent
City, got a room, scouted for for-sale land, bought a good plot, and . . . .

The other way to pass the 50 minute hour was to simply converse, to talk
as friends, or, at least, as acquaintances do. Just generally shoot-the-shit.
Sometimes not too casually; he had his opinions, I had mine. My heart,
you could say, was not inclined to bleed as readily as some orthodoxy
required. The good Doctor—he was a PhD—was, not surprisingly,
smart as hell and when need be—my need—the clever manipulator.

Back when we were getting to the core of the case, he asked, "Why this
hold over you? why did you have to do her bidding?"
That was a sore spot. "Well, when Belinda was, oh, less than a year-old, I
wasn't 'daddy' anymore; she wouldn't let me see her . . . anymore."
"You were daddy and then you weren't, why?" He stroked his chin and
gave it a pinch for emphasis.
"Finally, after calls and letters, she said that I'd had sex, maybe she said
an affair with Adriana who was a some-time baby-sitter."
"Did you?"
"Hell no, it never crossed my mind, I'd never . . . just never. It would have
seemed incestuous."
"That's ironic."

"Perversely so. I happened to run into Adriana at Peet's. She was pissed. Rita had had one of her hysterical fits. Adriana described her as 'crazy' and, I forget but there was much more emphatic language. She apparently was surprised as hell about that paranoid accusation—and mad about not just that, but losing her part-time gig."

"What happened to her, to Adriana?"
"I don't know, but much letter I got a wedding invitation from Barcelona. Of course it wasn't meant as an invite, just a nice gesture."
"That sounds . . . strange."
"I didn't think so, I just thought it was . . . nice."
"You think . . . maybe."
"It never occurred to me, she seemed so . . . nice."
Dr Maye pulled at his lower lip.

We were sitting in easy-chairs, not quite opposite each other. I could stare into space, the better to make those connections, or, with a slight turn, face him directly. We had abandoned our starting positions with he behind the desk of authority and the defendant on the office hot-seat.

"That was much later and she had your address?"
"I don't remember. She probably had it and my phone if there were any arrangements to be made . . . made about Bel." After sitting sad-faced, a pull on an ear lobe seemed to make the connection that "in fact, I remember, she was at my place with Bel once, for some reason. I don't remember but it was some reason or other."
"You just remembered that?" He clasped his hands behind his football-player neck.

"It was a long time ago . . . nothing much to remember. Isn't Rita's response a little paranoid? We hadn't had sex for . . . oh, I'd guess about a year and nine months and now this fantasy turns up. Very strange . . . and now she does a kind of unilateral custody action; a suspicion based on not much of either motive or opportunity."

.

"Suspicion or a bitchy bit of misinformation."

Chapter 8

"Memory is . . . of all the powers of the mind . . . the
most delicate and frail."
Ben Jonson

Life is lived chronologically. Well, more or less. The past and the
present may confuse the linear progression somewhat. Certainly
memories pay little attention to sequence; they form and inform both
arbitrarily and to our purposes. There are lacunae that can be filled;
other spaces are so blank as to be, seemingly, no longer a part of us.

The guy who wrote "Zen and Now" makes the point that we live with
one foot in the past and one in the future. We tend to lean, however,
quite naturally to our memories; as much as anything those ever-
passing phenomena *are* us. The present, quite perversely, is a gift not
fully appreciated. What ever goal is in mind, therapy is an exercise in
recollection. Or, perhaps, famously, recall is just "a labor in vain."
Implicit, however, in the therapeutic process, however it is facilitated
is: why not live in the present?

Early in that process, in a fit of ego-mania, I thought, this life, those experiences: a novel. So I joined that large population of would-be writers, 99% of whom will never see their hard-wrought words validated by a publisher's acceptance or payment. But I procrastinated. I filed that dubious aspiration to some barely accessible niche of my mind. I had also waited too long to build a house, and then only started that process when Belinda was lost to me. Then I started without knowing all that much about the actual construction. I had, however, lived in a house; I knew what it was about a house that I appreciated and what I could do with out. I've also lived in novels. But I was much less clear about the long story. Just how does the alchemy of structure and character and what-all-else envelope the reader in what you've put to page? To mesh the manner of, for just one aspect of such magic, the narration with the "what's it about" seems more akin to designing a machine of critical and moving parts than fixing a piece of this to a piece of that.

I don't have much imagination when it comes to characters. I can report what they do; I can infer from their actions; I cannot, however, concoct a character out of thin air. The narrator—that's me, Jeff Hodges— will be, of course, an ego-alterer. Others, from principals to walk-ons will have some resemblance to real people that is not exactly coincidental.

Chapter 9

"Experience is only half of experience."
Goethe

Luckily I gave up on education before my mind became numb and indifferent to to the larger and unknown world, before any inclination to learn and be involved in the pleasure and pain of ideas had been erased. And, of course, before I was certified as employable, educable and validated as a responsible citizen.

Perhaps it was bed-time stories that did it, that inclination to have some interest in the "whats" and "whys" of the world—and beyond. Just how my mother reading about talking animals and outrageously exaggerated exploits could be the cause of such an effect, well, I guess that such tales—told with serious humor—just might stimulate some stem cells of the mind.

It seems that about the time I started school that the family went through some sort of economic set-back, a crisis never talked about, never revealed. It did send my mother to work and subsequently Phil and myself. Not that we dropped out of grammar school or anything really Dickensian, but let's just say—as some field workers will tell you now—there were few if any eight-hour days. Farm labor was just what one did; some kids did it, others didn't. Not that I remember any of the latter doing anything as bourgeois as, say, going to summer camp. And, of course, farm kids did a hell of a lot more of it than us town kids.

Perhaps I rationalize, but those odd jobs and especially the stoop labor—those long rows and long days—provided more nourishment for the back bone than does now-a-days, no-school activities. And we made good spending money. I figured, for instance, that a day picking "pickles" would buy a pair of jeans with a lot left over to either save or fritter away. I'd guess that kids these days would consider such labor a bad career move. Can you imagine? Potato vacation! *Your not going to Disney Land, you're going to take a baloney sandwich and a bottle of pop and pick potatoes.* Not that it was put to us that way. It was, as I say, just what one did.

Mom and Dad were divorced. Well, not technically. They just didn't have that much to do with each other. They had a lot to do, it seemed that between them they were doing about four jobs. "How the hell am I supposed to sleep with that racket," Dad might yell at some after school rough-housing. He would be in bed after making a slaughter-house delivery and was trying to get some shut-eye before his grave-yard at the paper mill.

If the grown-ups had more work than play, we kids avoided the tedium that the former imposed and with a swarm of others equally demented with excess energy, we sledded down the steep drop winding down from the cemetery, or jumped into the pool that formed at the bottom of the old gravel pit, or, into challenging nightfall, improvised to the edge of delinquency.

But indoors, Karen, Alex, myself and Phil, the oldest and a rather benign
in loco parentis enforcer, enjoyed competitive and generally congenial game-
playing. We had our responsibilities and our squabbles, but the game was
the thing. Over the years we tired of Monopoly and then Scrabble was played
out. Alex tended to jump all over his Chinese Checkers opponents. Phil and I
were well matched in checkers. Karen dominated in gin. She was going to
learn bridge. "Let's get serious and put this kid's stuff behind us," the oh-
so-growing up sixth-grader scolded during a desultory game of euchre.
We had the four hands but it never came to that. The kid, however,
always knew how to play her cards.

Homework? I don't remember carrying anything to or from school
except sports stuff for one season or another. Except, and this had
nothing to do with any class, I had, for some reason checked out a
book of plays. It was a revelation for that seventh-grader to read, of
those I remember, "Arsenic and Old Lace," Tobacco Road" and "Of
Mice and Men." Could attending the actual staging of these been more
eye-opening? But reader that I was, the game was the thing. But I
don't think that those competitions prepared me for the larger and less
sporting game.

Before I graduated to that game, Wayne McCauley taught me chess. I'd
jogged—this was before anybody "jogged"—past the Post Office and
up the church hill to do a baseball card deal. But his checkered hard-
wood and exotic pieces promised a worldly arena of competition. But
this new game, this "war" game, was an up-hill battle. I didn't seem to
realize that study and memorization were required; there was a history
of standard openings and defenses; every game was not a new situation
that depended solely on your improvisational skill. Early in the clumsy

45

climb up the learning curve—playing against the few available opponents—many a match ended with the surprise check-mate. That cliché ending is not how real chess is played. Nor do real players generally play with fancy pieces on shiny wood. Slow learner that I am, I thought I was playing the real game by the time I got out of the Army. Then, later, at Berkeley, I got a graduate education that revealed my mediocrity and made it clear that I didn't have sufficient faculties to compete with serious tournament players. *The players who could discern the workings of a threat, deal with it and turn the tables.*

Chapter 10

"One's real life is often the life that one does not lead."
Oscar Wilde

"You got a driver's license?" Paul asked.

"Sure."

He threw me the keys to the Ford wagon and described the route I was
to take from Brainard to St Cloud: a round-about, long way-around so
as to hit a series of small towns. We, three like me, somewhat like me,
after, as one cynical "student" sales-guy expressed it, "selling slicks to
hicks," would then check into the Mizpah Hotel about supper time.

I didn't have a license. My driving experience probably could've been
measured, not in thousands but in dozens of miles.

"Mary needs some hits, needs to write some easy paper and get that
confidence. First natural territory you see, let her . . . just treat her right."

"Sure, OK." As if I was a competent agent in these matters.

"Here's the number of the hotel. Leave a message if . . . I don't think there's any Green River towns around here but if anybody gets put in jail . . . or anything, OK?" I put the "moderate rates" hotel card in my shirt pocket and took a look at the itinerary. Ah, the responsibilities of a crew chief. "Confidence, and be careful: no speeding."

In the outside word—the real out-on-your-own world—you can't go to the fridge and warm up some, say, some good beef stew. You have to pay for breakfast, for lunch, for supper and all the in between stuff. At home, all my life, I could just crap out in my bed, but I had put that kid's stuff behind. The deal is you have to pay to sleep in a bed.

I had to, not sing for my supper, but do a spiel. "Cold door" magazine sales is a tough way for any but the smoothest con-man—or con-girl —to make expenses. Not that I comb my conscience about such, but much later, I would wonder: how many of those "Boy's Life," Field & Stream," or "Time" subscriptions were made good on? Or, for that matter, a check was some-times not as good as it looked. Cash was preferred. Sometimes I didn't have breakfast money until the first cash sale and then there'd be no place to get as much as a Twinkie.

Why did I, one spring night, pack my gym bag, pocket my cash, step over Moose who gave me a quizzical look and a sleepy wag of his tail, and quietly leave my home through the never-locked kitchen door? I took a look back at the moon-lit little box of a white house, the dark windows framed by green, non-functional "shutters" and thought that was that for my home, for my family. I walked quickly the matter of minutes to get through town, hoping no one would notice this odd traveler. In the middle of the night there didn't seem to be soul astir, only one upstairs window bedroom window was aglow, the light shown softly from the

48

drawn shade. At a quickened pace I cut through a dewy pasture—the barbed wire too taut to slip through, so, at the post I climbed with extra care; I didn't want to present myself to the world with ripped pants—and hit the highway. I was like a thief-in-the-night, but why did I have to steal away?

The thing was, I wasn't escaping from home but from the damn high-school. But the school was blameless, as were the teachers, the kids. I wasn't the victim of any maltreatment. Not that in retrospect I'd give any sentimental endorsements. The fault didn't lie within that specific school; it was just that I couldn't abide any such situation, benign or otherwise. The fault lie within me; I had suffered the onset and continuation of a singular punishment: certainly no one else in the world was so afflicted. I'm sure that in the many intervening years that that malady has been identified and is probably treatable by some little pill. Back then it was an inexplicable—and untold—crippling caused by an unknown invader of the psyche or a faulty connection in the gray matter.

Who would I be without that malfunction? that deprivation that made some things impossible, critically so, definitively so and does so, to some degree, even now. I don't have the imagination to picture an alternative "me." But, in the end, was all that so bad? Maybe, similar to the cancer survivor who claims to be "stronger," or "a better person" for the experience, I've gained, again, some back bone by experiencing a sentence of alienation and loneliness: or, maybe not. My powers of insight aren't that great.

To explain to my parents that I had decided to forego the modest expectation of graduating high school would have been impossible.

Especially since rationally deciding isn't exactly what I did; I just fled.
Dropping out wasn't what kids in that school did. Oh, sometimes a girl
got pregnant and I'm sure there were others, but I don't remember. The
deal for kids like I was, was you graduated, went in one of the services, then
you probably had to go to the city to get a job, but married and settled; or
maybe you got unsettled and unmarried, but it was all going down some
narrow road of modest expectations. I certainly didn't think myself
superior to such a life.

Fortunately it turned out, some years later, that I was wrong about all the
leaving and being "the last of it." I did go home and it was all reconciling and
making good, but I was different and home was different; which was, is,
I guess, just the way life works: everything changes.

But, back to the other "road," there I was, a half-year after my leaving,
with considerably less cash and in another untenable situation. "Let's
quit," was the logical conclusion of a conversation between Mike, my
hotel roomie and myself. "Winter's coming, let's just head south," he
advised as he decisively stubbed out his rolled cigarette.
"I've got some white shirts in the laundry," I demurred.
"White shirts," he scoffed, "that's just excess baggage.
"Ya, you gotta point; I don't see us getting any shirt and tie jobs."
I'd just been promoted to driving the station wagon, but then I was going
to hit the road again. That time with a guy who looked more like a
muscular ex-con than a teen-age runaway.

"We'll tell Paul at breakfast and then check-out."
So, with ham and eggs in our bellies and not much in our pockets, we set
out hitch-hiking into that country known as The South.

Chapter II

"Death, the appointment we all must keep and
for which no time is set.
Charley Chan

"I didn't see no way out but getting out . . . out of town," Mike had
told me. Seems he'd knocked up a girl up in the iron-range country and,
though shy of liable for a statutory rap, he was down in the East Texas
Pineywoods country some where between what was called the "Sandy
Center" and the Trinity rivers with me, Shorty, BJ and Glenn, clearing a
swath through scrub oak—live oak? blackjack oak?—sawgrass and
fibrous undergrowth for an oil pipe line. I, like, somewhat like that
congenial absconder, could see no way out but to just get out; but I envied
his circumstances when he so off-handidly told about his tale. I had
never been in a position to do what he did.

But there he lay, all stained, drained and faded. His tanned arms were
like dull clay; his pissed-off expression paled to a dim and vacant
resemblance; his open road—a vague but ambitious path that he had

51

talked of—had ended in a way I'm sure he'd never thought about: in
the unforgiving dust and the sawed branches and sheared cuttings of our
sharp tools. We heard the higher revs of the motor just for maybe a
second or two and then it crashed to the ground and stalled. I'd heard a
surprised "sonofa . . ." and then saw the blood spurt, arc and then flow.
The chain had come apart and whipped across his neck; I guess it sliced
his jugular. He was about ten feet or so up an oak tree. Gaffs secured
his legs, but his upper body hung helplessly over the safety belt that held
him to the trunk. Glenn climbed up and put a tool-rag to the wound, but
then it was an ungainly and hurried chore getting his limp and leaden
body down. BJ knocked the gaffs loose and we slid Mike, one to another
until Shorty laid him down on hard ground. He was more than passed
out. Bood dripped from the still-green leaves.

On the table were two empty Lone Star bottles. Mike could usually pass
and we'd have a cold beer with our economy-class supper: a barbeque
sandwich, a burrito or maybe just a cold can of beans. There were four
socks drying over a lamp shade, a *Confidential* on the floor, Mike's
cigarette fixings were on the dresser—and what seemed incongruous
—his address book. The only addresses I had were where I was from
and where I was at. I thought I might be doing Mike a favor if I took
his lighter to that book: a minor incendiary incident to make for an even
cleaner escape. I thought later than it probably was just as well that I
didn't burn that little book.

It had been a tedious and hungry trip which ended, luckily, just outside
of Lufkin where Glenn and his crew gave us a lift. There had been one
interesting incident in, of all burgs, Hannibal, Missouri. I won't go into
it in case the police—if some oddity of statute or interest still applied

—might consider that cold case to be still on a back-burner. You never
know. We were in the right place at the right time that time and then
again when Glenn gave us a lift in his heavy-duty, tool and winch-
bedecked Dodge Power Wagon. It was good to get back to doing a man's
job.

For some reason, as if searching for the other occupant, I surveyed the
much-changed motel room. I thought of the man—from some
philosophical example?—who, alone in a room (a bare room? a
monk's cell?) would live more, by some criteria, than the man of action.
Then, later, what came to mind was: what an odd and beside-the-point
thought. But I was in a stunned state and not quite comprehending reality
to say nothing of meaning. I remember that I slipped a Max Schulman
paperback (I forget which one) into my packed bag, put my life's savings
in the watch-pocket of my jeans, swiped Mike's change from the dresser,
and made a getaway over to the Beaumont highway and stuck out my thumb.

"Where y'all headed?" the waitress asked as we parked our beat-up bags
and plopped ourselves at the counter. She couldn't have been much older
than we were but, solo, she was holding down that main drag oasis on
the graveyard shift. She had a name, but . . . . I do remember that she had a
Miss-Small-Town beauty. That was back in Hannibal. She'd kept our
coffee cups full and offered, several times, a Pall Mall; Mike accepted, I
declined. We were killing time until first light and then it was back on the
road.

"We don't know," Mike laughed. "we're just going til we get some kinda
job." She gave it some thought, but only had the discouraging word, "I
don't believe there's any work in this town."

53

Mike, I remember, came out of the Men's minus a healthy growth and his face all shinny. Our waitress swiveled her end-of-the-counter stool, danced her engaging blue eyes and said, "Make yerself ta home." We passed the slow predawn hours in the indifferent nighthawk light talking about this or maybe that in a round-about rhythm of earnestness, humor and teen-shy suggestiveness. Mike took the lead in that rambling-on of comforting conversation. The occasional customer, if I remember right, didn't break the sense of we three sharing a haven.

That's how I remember Mike, having an easeful and congenial time with cigarettes and coffee. And I remember our friend for a few middle-of-the night hours; her bemused and seemingly affectionate smile of course, but also that sexy, cheap, smudged-up and insubstantial white uniform that you don't see any more.

Chapter 12

*"Friendship is the marriage of the soul, and this marriage
is liable to divorce."*
Voltaire

Luke and I played ping-pong, 8-ball and chess, not especially expertly but very
competitively. One good thing about the army, well good and bad, was,
off-duty, there was always somebody around: Somebody to bullshit
with or somebody to compete against. Just like at home. During basic
at Fort Knox the firing range with an M-14 was game-on serious fun;
the bayonet drill, not so much. I gave the US Army three years; well
"gave" only as an alternative to being either drafted or a draft-dodger.
I got some dental work and I was given an honorable discharge. That
occurred just before the shit hit the fan in Vietnam. I did, incidentally,
do some good duty, but, frankly, I don't mention it much because my
job was clerk-typist. Dix, incidentally, was a big prison, both an army
stockade and a federal pen. I looked forward to civilian-free-as-a-
bird status, but I didn't feel confined. It never entered my mind that
I could ever be a resident of any type of total confinement.

I'd known Luke at Fort Dix as a conversational companion and a kickass competitor. Once, during a pick-up touch-football game, he laid a block on me that knocked me not just down but almost out. I thought for sure that I'd broken a rib or torn something or other. But, after taking inventory and enduring a few diagnoses and different degrees of concern from my various-sized play-mates, I woozily continued, but I don't think I was the QB's first option any more.

That evening I was lying on my bunk reading "Auntie Mame" (I thought myself impervious to ridicule; I was never tested) when Luke came by and took a seat on my foot-locker. "How're you feeling?" he asked.
"Not bad, it wasn't a very large truck."
He smiled appreciatively. "I'm sorry I knocked the shit outa you."
"Nothing to be sorry about, it was a clean hit."
"But a *palpable* hit."
Yes, it certainly was. My mind reached to return his serve and said, "But not a poisoned one."

We'd kept in touch as army-buddies rarely do. When I was in New York, I took him up on an offer of an over-night. In Chinatown for dinner, Luke enthused over his post-army life. I couldn't match his optimism. He'd walked into a gallery, talked, I guess, quite artfully and got a job that was right up his alley. I didn't begrudge him his luck, but by fortune cookie time his presentation of that luck was getting tiresome.

He lived at a curious and fortuitous address: a freight-elevator access warehouse above the Soho gallery where he was probably the primary

mover of large objects. He was also a painter. I remember him alluding
to something called minimalism and various phenomena from the
insular "art world." He had his "in" but I don't know if he ever made a
name for himself. I never saw his name, but I imagine there are artists
who do well who never come to the attention of those of us who pay
little mind to that arbitrary business.

One corner of that attic-to-end-all-attics was, very minimally, his bedroom,
studio and some plumbing. Those quarters were admirably strange
and unconventional, but it was the surrounding clutter that was notably
odd. Canvases hid there as if understandably reluctant to go downstairs;
transgressive and agitprop pieces went underground up there;
very grotesque Koons-like animalistic creations ballooned like
some Macy's Day parade rejects; delicate and vulnerable creations were
squeezed by plaster and ceramic concoctions; mechanical and electronic
devices spilled their guts: all the leavings of dealing. Intrusive street
light made for shadows that loomed ominous and boogie-man-like.

"I've got his number, I'll look it up in the morning."
Sure, I thought, like I give a shit. We were camped in cozy-corner. My
bedding, over, under and pillow, was moving-van pads. Not bad.

When, in the constraints of uniformed life and ignorant of our ignorance,
we meddled freely and sportingly in affairs of the mind. Not diligently,
not studiously, but still . . . In downtown Manhattan, however, the
difference between us was not complimentary: it was irritating. But
Luke seemed oblivious; I had changed—who doesn't when reaching
civilianhood—but he seemed some sort of Dean Moriarity, which was
quite a change. I didn't know it then, but he may have been on speed;

but at any rate we were on obviously different frequencies. On top of which, which seemed to be not compatible with his new hyper-self, he was on a Gurdjieff/Ouspensky kick.

"You'd get along."
I grunted and adjusted my pale-rose pillow.
"He's always questioning, he knows how to get to the heart of the matter, to the reality beyond perception."
Ya, I thought, a "seeker,"
"He read philosophy at Trinity College, but you know . . ."
"Trinity Dublin?"
"Trinity Cambridge . . . or is it Oxford? With Godsley, Gomes, Godie, some big name . . ."
"Doesn't ring a bell," not that anybody from any Trinity would.
". . . but you know . . . it isn't an integrating process . . . . there's no path, no real road to the True Self."

I can't say that I knew what that *true* self was. Not that I'd given it much thought but "selves" keep changing, they over-lap, relapse and sometimes collapse. Some who do think about such would say that it's difficult to say what a "self" is, to say nothing of a "true self."

Kurt Vonnegut said, "Be careful about who you pretend to be; you'll turn into that person." Well, there is a difference between pretending and emulation, but I'd guess that the most common threat to authenticity is "belief." Maybe even the "belief in belief."

The next day I boarded bound for Amsterdam, the Belgian freighter "Vingt."
What was I seeking? Who was I emulating?

Chapter 13

*"Why not seize pleasure at once? How often is happiness
destroyed by preparation, foolish preparation."*
Jane Austen

A funeral procession came by. It was simple, dignified and very matter-
of-fact. No limousine, no cars, no hearse, in fact, no casket. We were in
the Zoco Chico having a mint tea in the cool winter sun, just watching
the passers-by when that modest procession of men entered the square.
The six in the lead carried on their shoulders what could only have been
a corpse, a shrouded corpse. They, in mostly gray djellabas, moved as if
they were mumbling ghosts; they did no wailing, no keening or prayerful
emoting. They were on their way, by one of the Medina alleys that
radiate from that unsquare square, to one of the cemeteries on the out-
skirts of Tangier.

The previous morning we had been in bed, Veronique and me in her
sunny room on the Rue Rembrandt, when the building shook. The
obvious observation was made. Later we learned—do I remember
that accurately?—that a fisherman had died in that minor earth-quake.

I do remember, among a half-dozen of us at a back table in Dean's bar, that English writer who looked more morely than Robert Morley. He kept on, of all things, about the Marquis of Queensbury. Veronique just nursed a bottle of *Speciale*. A dotting of freckles called coy attention to her flirty playfulness. Well, she had that but she also had a depth of emotion that I was too callow to understand, too shallow to appreciate. That night, after some banter and some mutually appreciative eye-play, she, while holding my gaze, stood up, put on some foreign-army fatigue jacket, picked up her tote bag and cast her gray-green eyes door-ward. The pick-up was so exquisite that, as if I were a puppet, I picked up on it and rose from my chair. She took my arm and we exited Dean's as casually and decorously as some still-compatible couple leaving church.

"I don't know, I just do . . . sometimes." She was crying. We'd fucked and she was crying. I'd never seen that, making love and crying, but with my experience there was much that I hadn't seen. I didn't know then that later I'd shed a few tears of self-pity over the ending of it with enigmatic Veronique.

"I could try to explain," she said, "but, I don't know . . ."
"That I'd understand?" I didn't and I didn't say any more.
"How could you? maybe you would?"
She laid her head on my chest, her tears matted my hair and trickled down my side. The sheet was wet with our sweat and all. I stroked her hair and pulled it gently from her face. We lay like that until the tears subsided.

Veronique looked up at me, a fiery melancholy from deep within her eyes and asked, "Do you know why they call it the 'little death?'"

What the hell was she talking about. I confessed, "No, I don't."
"It's as if you leave your body, you leave your mind, yet at the same
time, body and mind are by some fusion, the same thing." Wow,
explosive, I had no idea of what to say. "Maybe" she explained, "to
be both the experience and the sensate *experiencer* is to be on the edge,
the edge of ecstatic nothingness." Then, as if to disavow any
pretentiousness, she, almost apologetically, smiled. While I have only
a vague recollection of what went on for hours previously, I still have
that fleeting glint of a smile expressed by those moist green eyes; green
flecked eyes tinged with a shadow; eyes that like some only imagined
gem, had both a deep luster and, through her tears, a sparkling refraction.

She was much more traveled than I was; maybe we were from
different planets. She'd had forays off the "blue" highways or no
highways and, among other routes, across North Africa. She'd ventured
with curiosity and, to hear her tell it, with little trepidation almost in
the tradition of those Victorian lady-adventurers but some-what before
the swarming hordes of western Katmandu-ers and Bali-highers. She
had been at Mass General and her native Belfast, an ICU nurse; she
knew about the edge.

Much later it came to me why Veronique hadn't the inclination to
continue our somewhat exotic Mediterranean affair: I was a poor lover
and a less than interesting companion. I didn't fulfill her, what?
emotionally, intellectually, vaginally? I know that my cup had runneth
over. Was I becoming dimly aware that I had a hell of a lot to learn.
Were there emotional dimensions that I had no idea of? Were there
qualities of women that I failed to perceive? Why had that woman
left me longing and needing to possess? Did I, at that time, actually

61

ask myself these questions? or did they come to me later as part of the retroactive and retrospective construction of the self?

But that was just an affair; was love involved in what was obviously a transient involvement? Certainly it was true that I was nothing but a man and she was, in a primal and mystical sense, something of a woman.

Well, at any rate, I had paid my fare with a stack of street-business dirhams and was on the manifest for—when ever that happened to be— the next Yugolinea vessel to make port and bound for any US port.

Chapter 14

"War is the game the world so loves to play."
Jonathan Swift

"It was just one of those training accidents." "They died?" she asked.
"Stokes, well, I won't describe it, but, ya, there wasn't any doubt. He was a friend of sorts. The other guy never saw him but we heard that he recovered . . . or, at least that he survived." Cathy grimaced and looked down at her hands clasped so tightly that the knuckles protruded and the fingers of each hand dug into the back of the opposite hand. "But that was kid's stuff compared to Nam. I don't know if I could've taken the real thing."

I could have shot the "gooks," that's what they were to our guys; trouble is you see a gook or is he just some guy? or is that kid just a gook kid or is he trouble? Some guy, just a kid himself, comes into country thinking he's defending the good from some bad. Pretty soon he learns he's fighting the *Vietnamese*, or that every gook that isn't ARVN is suspect; the only thing he's defending is himself and his unit. I couldn't take that shit. I could've survived my guys being *offed* or *greased;* what I probably couldn't take was the *suffering.* The suffering of . . . well, most everybody . . . kids. I was thankful and a little guilty that I wasn't there, but I didn't even consider that I could suffer: not horrible gut shot, shattered bone, burned suffering. Punji sticks!

Cathy looked at me quizzically, as if she'd understood what I had explained to myself. Did she look with empathy? commiseration? or just curiosity? What was the war to her? an occasion for an anti-authority pep rally?

"What would you have done?" she asked.

What would I have done? "I hope I would have had the guts not to go."

I drank my tea to stall for coherence. "Jeez . . . well . . . . if I was still in the army would've been a much more difficult decision."

"That's, I guess," Cathy said, "what makes these guys believe . . . . you just can't believe that you're on the wrong side."

"I don't know if it's a matter of sides, right or wrong."

Cathy tilted her head in questioning disappointment. Her mouth tensed and her luminous blue eyes iced over. "You see those coffins, that daily list of the dead, that body count, if that isn't about right and wrong I don't know what is . . . it's about morality."

I just nodded in agreement. "But for the guys in country, especially for the drafted guys, it's more a matter of survival . . . just plain old survival."

"But some," she said, "isn't that the situation?—need to believe, need to rationalize their situation."

We could have speculated about why young men, willingly or not, will follow a leader, follow a crowd, follow some dubious reason to fight their neighbor or invade some faraway land, but it's been standard procedure, I'm sure, for all of history.

"But you're right, some believe in the mission and, well, others have a pretty good idea that they're not stopping those dominoes; or defending the folks in Santa Barbara, San Clemente, Whittier . . . where ever. It all goes back to 'who lost China.'"

"Lost China, I didn't know China got lost." Facetious, of course, but had she even heard of the "China Lobby" or Dienbienphu? Was she one of those who knew what the hell they were anti-warring about? or was she just another anti-war camp follower?

"Or, some," I pontificated, "would say JFK handled the missile crisis, LBJ had to have the balls to handle this . . . this supposed commie threat." i
I was at Dix then and we were on alert for a month. I didn't want to go on with any "war" stories, especially since that episode was as near as I came to any war. Much later I'd had my doubts about that crisis and I wouldn't be surprised if it was more about JFK's political crisis than a real Soviet threat. But I didn't want overload Cathy's attention with a conspiracy speculation.

But Cathy seemed to consider my sophisticated briefing adequate and in a gesture of relaxed summation, she stretched her tennis-tanned arms and reached her palms toward the ceiling. Then she raised her cup and said, "Here's to our little contribution . . . and to our health."

Of course I was against the war, but was I "anti-war"? hell, no. But, back then I was going to make common cause with many who were still berating Truman for ending a war.

Governor Reagan called out the National Guard. The Oakland police and the CHP were there to help the Berkeley and campus cops. Streets were barricaded, south of campus was a tear-gassed war zone. Somebody was going to get killed. It wasn't Chicago '68, but —standard procedure—zealous anti-warriors baited and threatened police who were only too ready and able to reciprocate with superior force.

It was more than enough for me; just to show up made the point. A straw-haired young man had his head two-toned with blood. A gray-haired woman sat on the curb, holding her head as if to keep invasive reality out. I grabbed her arm, "Let's get out of here." She shook me off vigorously as if I was part of the attack that had apparently shocked the hell out of her. Or maybe she was intent on sitting civil disobedience. I just skedaddled over Telegraph, continued west past the Blake Street Hawkeye's Theater where I first saw Cathy, then zigzagged north and west to my place near St Joseph the Workman.

But that escape brought up a disturbing question: what would I do in real combat? Combat where an enemy wasn't just a uniformed force that just wanted you to disperse. I dispersed. In combat exercises I had done pretty well; it was even enjoyable in a testing Yourself kind of way. But that was kid's stuff, a death here, a death there, *kid's stuff.*

"They rounded up a bunch on Oxford and took them to Santa Rita."
It was Cathy on the phone. "Ya, I'm OK, I'm . . . . OK, lungs got a little burned but I'll be fine. But Zach got clubbed across the shoulder and it doesn't look good . . . all swollen and purply, but we're guessing nothing broken. But we're lucky compared to I guess it was an SDS crew, they got the shit beat out of them."

Brave Zach, anti-war hero: And Cathy his Nightingale. Thankfully. it wasn't her nicely-formed and fair body that got all purply.
"You should meet; you've got a lot in common."
"Like yourself? Now you know that you're very uncommon."
"Oh, do I detect a little insecurity?"
"Oh, a scosh," I said to humor her. I didn't want to do a back-and forth with her and make myself vulnerable to good-natured but ill-feeling quips. Not that Cathy's response would be scripted. She didn't have that tape-in-the-head that most of us have. She'd been an understudy and got to do a few Ophelias at the Santa Cruz Shakespeare. Making that poor girl credible would seem to require inner strength: strength to appear innocent, used, confused and then, mad as a hatter, drowning with her flowers. Maybe the discipline needed to give yourself over to a difficult role—to play make-believe for real—

strengthens the psychic structure of one's authenticity. Then, again, it's obvious that such role-playing does no such thing for some, be they actors or we playing the audience.

"But Zach's not insecure, are you Zach?"

The patient apparently replied with a spirited witticism. I could hear Cathy's appreciative Laughter.

"Zach's in pain; I'm icing him down."

I passed on the obvious and said something even dumber, "I thought everybody in the theater was insecure. Isn't that the explanation for strutting your stuff?" i

"Jeffer-ree, that's a moldy old myth. But I could do some *strutting* if the role called for it."

"I'm sure you could, just like . . . oh . . ."

"Gwen Verdon."

Cathy's moves were serpentine and sinuous but defined and expressive of the rockin' blues that moved us. She was a *dancer.* Once at Eli's—it may have been the time we expressed our condolences for the recently late Eli to his cashier-wife—a rather senior black fellow told us with innocent emphasis, that we danced *just like them.*

"Beausoleil at Ashkanaz," I reminded, "Saturday night."

"Spell it, no, I'm looking forward, ya, after a few curtain calls, ungunk my face and come down a little, ya, we could make the second set most of it."

Chapter 15

"Life is too short to be small."
Disraeli

"'Suicide Cafe.' That's one of my shorts: doesn't this place . . . ?"
His question was not exactly apt. The "Med" was populated, it seemed,
by uber-Berkeleyites. Granted, a few may have have been excessively
world-weary. But it also seemed a civil haven from the post-hippie
pall and degradation that was already apparent on the Avenue.

"Not that I knew if . . . ?" Zach observed, "but it seems to be the place
where a suicide would hang out." I took out my cigarettes and laid the
pack on the table. "Smoke?" "Oh, a Sherman's," he said and I did the
minor ceremony of providing fire; we both inhaled deeply with
satisfaction. Someday, they say, such public satisfaction will be against
the law; my after dinner smoke will have to be a private affair. Cathy
didn't join us.

"What do you think Cathy, will hanging out here make us dangerously depressed?"

"Not me," she told me with an airy smile of feigned cheerfulness."

Well, she wanted me to meet her director. "A fascinating guy, he knows Shakespeare characters that I've never heard of. He even knows that old Greek and Roman stuff, you know, 'Midsummer Night's' and those old plays." Since I didn't know a thing Greek or Roman about Shakespeare, I thought I'd keep my mouth shut on the general subject. And I thought at the time, sure, boring as hell but then again I might learn something. From such "experts," I'd learned, among other things, not to be intimidated by those who know more than I do.

"These dopios may make us manic, but hardly depressed," she offered. We three were sipping double espressos. I reached over, in a gesture of possession and affection, brushed her hair aside—that fair hair suffused with a tawny under-tone—and lightly traced two fingers down the nape of that supple neck.

"But I get ideas here," Zach continued on his sad cafe theme. "It's not a 'all the lonely people' scene, but you can—I can, anyway—pick up on what's going on inside some of the more transparent heads". We were in the balcony, from that vantage Zach could mine material. Nice work, I thought, if if you can get it. *If you can get it.*

"Those two, ya, those two maybe lovers," Cathy responded to Zach's omniscience, "aren't they an attractive couple?" I glanced down, "Adorable." "I can't see them." Zach observed, "tell me their story."

Cathy and I looked at each other. Who can tell a story about two young people in conversation at a cafe? be they attractive or lovers or attractive lovers or whatever. Well, telling a story is one thing; telling their story, that's another story.

"You don't have eyes in the back of your head?" Cathy asked.
"No eyes, no radar, no ESP."
"She's fiddling with a pen," Cathy observed, "there's a small notebook on the table, as if she's going to write something but they're talking, very casually with pauses. As if they're considering what to say or they're just comfortable and feel no need to be responsive. It's definitely not a first date."

My cup was dry, the cigarette expired. I didn't want to try and infer what was going on in the those opaque but attractive heads. "They won't notice you," I told Zach, "see what you can see." He declined a peek. He seemed intent on getting his actors to use their imagination, or did he just want to play the role of "The Magus"?

"He's doing the cocked head, trying to express . . . ," Cathy wouldn't guess.
"It's like silent film," Zach informed, "the action tells, the expression tells." We fell silent at that profundity. He continued, "Look at radio, I mean, the old-time radio drama. You see it because of the expression of the voice. That's what I like about theater; to all that the audience adds another dimension; an engaged audience is part of the creation."

Cathy added, "Ya, if you don't get the audience coming along with you, you're in trouble."
"And in the theater," Zach added an exaggeration, "it doesn't take about

71

a hundred pages to get the audience on board." We paused to take in the hundred pages. He continued, "That's the trick, you enlist the audience and to do that you need to project confidence; even if you're playing shaky and nervous, you have to be confident that you're playing shaky and nervous."

"Just like George Burns said about sincerity, if you can fake that you've got it made," Cathy added with a fake self-deprecating grin.
"You ever do that Cathy?" he asked, "lose it?"
"You mean *lose it,* lose it?"
"Ya, major melt-down, major freeze?"
Cathy didn't answer; she just gave him her full baleful.
I remember thinking, interesting shop-talk, but . . . .

The couple got up to leave. She did a theatrical wrap-around with her shawl; he pulled the collar of a heavy sweater over his handsome neck. We could see them, outside, embrace and then. somewhat awkwardly, kiss.
"I told you," Zach said, "there was antipathy there."
I didn't know if he was serious, delusional or just facetious. I looked at Cathy, she just smiled confidently as if she knew what Zach was being so insightful about.

Later I asked Zach about his "Suicide Cafe." I figured if it was published he would've mentioned some esoteric Review or other. We were in a yuppie-ish brew-pub with a clientele somewhat different than that of the Mediterranean Cafe. None of this crowd seemed to be ponderers of suicide, or, for that matter, maybe not much of any matter. But, of course, one never knows. Was Zach mining material here?

"It's really about not committing suicide."

"As opposed to 'not about' committing suicide?"

He nodded, "Exactly, a distinction with a difference."

My head expanded at this and I reproached myself for allowing this pretentious twit to have that effect. But, double reproach: why was I characterizing him so invidiously? Jealousy? And, besides, some of the most interesting people are a phonies.

"It's written in the first person," he revealed.

"So, this main character . . . ?"

"Ever walk out of the LA bus station down on Main, some place down there, after a long trip?"

"Just so happens . . ."

"I try to combine that feeling with a good mix of old-time existential malaise and the dreary aspects of contemporary . . . ah, cafe society. This guy gets off the bus—any town, any place—he's feeling all scummy from a couple of days of recycled air, his appetite has been shot-to-hell by depot food—you know the feeling. He's alone in the depressing part of town. He gets a bleak hotel room, showers in a moldy stall and dries off with a thread-bare towel—you get the picture." "I get the picture."

"The set-up is desolation row; he ends up at a place called "Suicide Cafe.""

"Where the customers ask themselves 'do I have a cup of coffee or do I kill myself?'"

"Precisely," as he indulged in an unguarded smile.

"Then," I guessed facetiously—a good rule of thumb being to know just how far to go and then go a bit farther—"they were waiting for Hickey to bring the ice."

"Precisely the opposite," Those characters were living a hopeful

73

delusion; these habitués are voluntarily hopeless; Hickey, the savior, turns out to be a perverse rationalizer; my narrator is an innocent, he's not a Candide but a level-headed guy who, maybe not consciously, but he recognizes the absurdity of the 'life is absurd' school."
"Well, that sounds impressively counter-literary."

His darkly stubbled (this was before *that* look) pale face smiled—as if he was trying to think something. He raised his glass of Guiness-colored brew and I clinked with my lager. Not a bad guy.

"Medium rare, no mayo," interjected a fellow with a heavy-duty apron. Our sandwiches had arrived. That was a "happen-to-run-into" meeting. Zach, with a long-legged push of the chair opposite him had played the host with a "have a seat, pardner."

"Don't suppose you ran into Burroughs in Tangier?" he asked.
"No, nor the Bowles or Barbara Hutton. You a Burroughs reader?"
"'Junkie' was good."
"Ya, that's about it. Another beer?"
"No thanks," he said, "let's go to the Strada for a coffee and a smoke."
"How's the shoulder?"
He made an elaborate slo-mo pitching motion with his right arm. "It takes more than one hit to keep me down . . . and out."

Chapter 16

*"The art of being happy lies in the power of extracting happiness
from common things."*
Henry Ward Beecher

"When I got out of the Army I got on that Amsterdam-bound freighter,"
I told Cathy while trying to keep a revealed itinerary from wandering too
boringly into our time together. Well, not straight out. There was about a
year of looking for a job, getting laid off from jobs, working temp or day
labor at forge, foundry and various uninspiring factory assignments. I made
a little union-wage money at American Can out in Milwaukee's north side
and then—American canned. The big union-wage factories on the south-
side didn't seem to want anybody with my much too geographically varied
resume. Or, maybe, they just didn't want anybody—and those days, I
read later, were the "good times."

So, I decided to take a vacation from the hard work of looking for a job.
Way back then it didn't take much. Two peseta wine and free tapas, for
instance, made your exchange in Barcelona buy time, that most valuable
of commodities.

Cathy had, of course, been to Europe. She'd enjoyed a junior semester in Florence. Now any encountered Italian was a chance to go back, lingually, to the old country. She'd made a pot of tea and we were sitting in her, well, her shared kitchen on Bienvenue overlooking Willard Park. The park where she was my exclusive tennis instructor and primary practice partner.

She sliced thick slices of banana bread for us. "You bake it?" "Taste it." I took a good bite and tried to discern an answer. "Nice spice, a little ginger, moist with a *very* nice mouth-feel, of all the banana bread bakers in . . ." She affectionately throttled me.

"No, I paid. By then the work-away was a romantic delusion."
"I paid Air-Italia and it was quite romantic—both ways."
"As was, I imagine, living *la dolca vita* in Florence."
"Oh, *you* could imagine. It was, oh, a little too touristy and sweaty but very good for sweet memories and for the senses, several of them." Then, as if some memory or another had intruded, she pursed her lips and knotted her brow. "Well there were a couple of sour incidents, being so blond, I guess."
"Jeez, especially being so fetchingly blond and . . . so much more; ya, I can . . . well, I can't imagine." I took her hand, the slightly callused one and we just sat for a while with that soft connection, that comforting and casual binding.

"What were you studying? besides the sense of things?"
"Studying? Oh, ya, being Italian, I guess, you?"
"Looking, looking around, sitting and looking, lotsa walking around and just looking. I'm a good looker."

It was colder'n hell in Amsterdam, so after a few weeks I headed south. But not before, with ship-mates Beth and Gary, we visited the Van Goghs, the

Rembrandts, Anne Frank's, the Amstel Brewery and—oh, yes, but solo—

one or two of those whore houses with the display windows. I listed, in that

order, those cultural high-lights for Cathy. She gave me the dubious chin-

tucked, eye-brows raised look. "One *or* two? You don't remember one or two?"

"Well, three, if you want to get specific."

She humphed a dismissive laugh and poured more tea. I watched those very

adept hands tip the terra cotta pot. *The way you pour my tea, will their be a*

memory of all that. She was sure and steady in those minor chores; Cathy

made no busy or superfluous moves, she was elegant in motion as well as

feature. Those lips, for instance, more than ample but well-defined with a

promise of a smile; sometimes, however, they could be belittling and

bitter and when angry they would purse shrewishly.

"I'm sticking with the one-hand back-hand," I informed.

"To each his own."

"There's nothing more elegant in sport than a good *one-hand*, top-spin

back-hand."

"You aspire to elegance?"

"Of course," I dead-panned.

"I always thought of you as a function man."

We drank from clear glass cups that revealed the dark and honeyed brew.

She had, from that corner shop on Telegraph of many jars of esoteric dried

vegetation, gun-powder tea and peppermint leaves: Moroccan mint tea. Not

quite as good as I remembered but now standard fare. We rested our cups

in the warming sun from the west window that slid across the formica table.

Cathy reached across the table and took my hand as if to do a palm-reading and traced her forefinger from the tip of my right middle-finger down maybe a life-line to the wrist. "You've got soft hands." I questioned her with a look. "I mean soft John McEnroe hands, soft Ozzie Smith hands." I'll take that; a few more attributes and I'd be a hell of a player.

I had some "ball sense' from way back when I had, figuratively, hung up my spikes. While my reflexes adjusted to speed, I thought that even if I didn't become "one hell of a player," that I'd be, some lucky day, one of that cohort of retired guys with year-round tans who played often for serious fun: another good game. It didn't work out so golden-agey.

From the kitchen window we could see two players who rallied with confidence and continuity. We could hear the solid "bock" of each well-struck ball. On the other court a young couple flailed away, all wristy, no solid play. The erratic trajectory of their weak balls didn't provide a connection. They didn't cover the court as much as traips all over it retrieving feeble net-balls and unreturnable wild shots.

"Too bad you didn't start as a kid and . . ."
"In my dotage."
"Ya, what ever your dotage, you do-it-age is."
"You started . . . ?"
"Junior High."

I didn't know it at the time—who does?—that I was at the top of my game, generally speaking. Even in tennis, with encouragement from my partner I was enjoying steady improvement. Perhaps my upgrade from learner to player came when I took a set quite decisively from Cathy.

I started, winning the first three points while spinning in the first serve to
get it in play; at 40-love the serve was flat with a-little-reverse-twist; the
slight curve of the ball bringing it just inside the "T." Cathy could only
watch the ace whiz by. She asked when we changed ends, "Where did
you get *that?*" I was working swing-shift and getting in a lot more
practice than she could afford me.

Later I was beating youngsters half my age who had been playing
a good decade more than I had. Well, maybe that was literally true only a
time or two, but I make my point.

Chapter 17

"It isn't premarital sex if you have no intention of getting married."
George Burns

Rita was sitting in the student union lounge. I'd played chess there, but that get-to-gether was to be more serious than mock warfare. It was the first of a series of "we have to talk" meetings. I didn't think until much later, why were these important conferences always on neutral territory? How far back did her association with BAWAR (Bay Area Women Against Rape) go? We had had the last of our mutually desirous, very together get-to-gethers. She sat, as if deep in thought, her hands uncharacteristically folded in her lap.

"Hi," I only put my hand on hers; we were at the end of it. I expected a "not see each other anymore" scene. I was thinking 'so long, it's been good to know you.' She looked up at me with sad and beseechingly serious gray-blue eyes, hesitated and said, "I'm pregnant."

I reacted, I imagine as many a man has done in such a sobering situation. I was stunned; my feelings were an unsortable confusion. What my mind did distinctly register, however, was that I was put-upon and put-out. How dare she? I hugged her. I didn't feel any "we're in this together" response.

I asked gently, "Do you want the baby?"
Without hesitation, she said, "Yes, I do."
"Do you want me to be the daddy?"
She pinned me with a soulful look. "Yes."

My confusion floundered; what is the protocol here? Should I have said, "It's *your* baby. I'll kick in a little, but it's *your* baby." Should I have tried to wash my hands of all but minimal financial responsibility. The joy and ineffable love to come was unexpected; but the pain and disappointment were also unexpected. I should have seen the latter coming, but as I've said, I'm a slow learner. Years later Rita would give emotional testimony that I had pressured her to have an abortion.

Years earlier I had been ascending stairs behind Rita. That prospect was promising. And then there was that first look into somebody's quarters which is always interesting—and indicative. Maybe especially so when you expect to be in bed with them. Well, as the saying goes, be careful what you wish for.

Rita turned on a swing-arm lamp over a drafting table. The light revealed a real mess, but a business-like industrial mess. "I told you I was a painter," she explained. The floor was a splattered drop-cloth,

smeared shelves held tubes of acrylic and cans of brushes. Stretched
canvases were lined up in a rack. Finished or works in progress?
From what I could see, I didn't see, just then, making an art inquiry.

When she pulled back a curtain we were in a very different room.
"This is where I live, that was where I work," she told me. Low and
soft lamp light illuminated the two of us, I imagine, to our mutual
advantage. Potted flowers were on a sill; a desk exhibited a vase of cut
blue iris. A generous-sized bed was covered with a flowered fabric.
All very homey. No—thank god—Buddhas, graven images, gurus,
cats or hippie-like art or artifacts. We settled in after a tentative and
then avid "getting to know you" process; settled was that the inviting
bed was, for then, taken off the table.

"Church, really?" I hadn't been, except for two weddings at the
Unitarian, since . . . . "My friend Issy, Izabella, she's from Valencia, she
wanted some company. I took it as a sort of anthro field trip."
"Was it trippy?"
"In a way, but I expected Latin. I don't exactly keep up with . . . ."
"What, no Latin? what am I supposed to do with *susipiat dominus
sacraficium et . . .* , etcetera, etcetera?"
"What does that mean?"
"I have no idea."

Several days later we lay on that bed, quite spent and making only
lazy and comforting touches. In an innocent gesture, I leaned over
and kissed her luxurious pelt of pubic hair. Rita put on her glasses
and peered into my eyes as if to discern what was on the other side
of those eyes she barely knew. Her smile, framed by a strong jaw-

line, was generous. She got up, handed me a box of kleenex, put on
a kimona and asked, "To drink?" Her bare-foot walk revealed her
slight limp, but it was barely noticeable . . .

"Oh, something cool and clear, like water."
Sometimes, before going out to a once-in-a-while dinner, we'd have
a vodka and something and split a joint. In her line of work she had
access; she knew people. One of those times she asked about LSD.
"Oh, yes, it's coming back to me. You haven't . . . ?"
"No, I've just wondered. But, seriously, what did you . . . ?"
"I took it seriously; it is a trip . . . can be a dangerous trip."
"That doesn't tell me much; dangerous, sure, but what did you . . . . ?"

I poured a little more vodka into my iced tonic and tried to imagine
just how the hell does one explain the inexplicable? "The first thing,
I'd say is, do it with the right people, just one or two and certainly not
alone."
"That sounds like . . . like something of an intimate ritual. And who
knows who the 'right' people are?"
"I guess you never *really* know. It's just that it's safer, like on any
trip, if you go with somebody who's been there and knows the lay of
the other-land, the Perelandra." Rita sloshed her glass, sipped and said,
"You don't make it sound too enticing. And what's this Perelandra?"
"Oh, just a literary allusion . . . just a compensatory quirk. It is,
if I remember right, quite apt, but I just want to make the point that it's
not a casual and getting blasted thing to do; it's the opposite of that."
"You know I wouldn't think like that."

No, I knew she wouldn't, "But the thing is, once you're on your way there is no such thing as rational thinking; you leave that mind; you leave your sensible perception and . . . you may come close to some indefinable edge. Well, maybe, it's different for everybody; maybe it's different each time. I should know but . . . . I don't know."

She gave me a rap on the head and said, "You still haven't described what you saw, what you experienced.' I took a drink and tried to formulate a coherent response. "It's beyond my powers of description. But you're visual, maybe you'd see colors and . . . *manifestations* that are unreal or maybe more than real. Maybe from some pre-conscious; it's something so subjective that language can't cope with it—not with any accuracy."
"Deep," she said and feigned an exasperated smile.

I never knew her age or her birthday. I was, I guess, about a dozen years. older. I didn't delude myself about "love' and such complications. I didn't think she did either. I was, in effect, exploiting her: I her and she me. Rita was a competent professional woman and a feminist and an artist. I was not stringing her along with the slightest hint of "some-day." Certainly marriage or living together was never mentioned— by either of us. Fact is—and this is so cruel—she was a "place-holder."

I was on the rebound from Cathy. I wouldn't say that she'd broken my heart, but something was broke, disconnected and dysfunctional. It is a novelistic convention for men in that state of romantic despair, that indulgent funk, to fuck around. How do they do it? Morose men, drinking too much (another standard procedure) are making out serially with women who are attracted to . . . what? Mostly, I'd guess, the projections of middle-age male novelists.

So I wasn't keeping up with prescribed standards of behavior, but other interests were—as I understood our affair—not proscribed. There were out-side liaisons, but there was nobody to induce, seduce or tempt me—or accept me—from what I thought was an uncomplicated and mutually satisfying relationship. And I was sure she thought what I thought until, for what ever reason, she had second thoughts.

One accusation that Rita never made was that I didn't marry her. I never suspected such an aspiration; but it's only a natural suspicion that maybe the pregnancy was supposed to seal a deal. And it's only natural, even for me, to have some sympathy for the dread of that bio-clock running down. Later I heard, maybe just a rumor, that Rita had had her IUD removed.

Chapter 18

"There are three kinds of women in the world, two are griefs, and one is a treasure to the soul."
Rumi (The Sheikh Who played with Children)

"**I thought it was tomorrow—and it certainly was,** that was the plan. But there they were, Rita and Belinda ringing the bell. Bel jumped into my arms with an endearing "Daddy." Then she saw Judy, as did, of course, the trailing Rita. She would have greeted Judy in similar fashion, if less athletically. But she knew; she knew that any such enthusiasm would not sit well with her mother. Belinda passed little information from home base, but it was obvious that selective info was carried back to Modesto. Carried, but how innocently, how unintentionally? What was the tone of that intel, what effect did it have on Rita? Perhaps only a minor bother, but it may have been an aggravating major frustration; it may have been the realization that she wasn't the only maternal influence on our daughter.

Luckily Judy and I were dressed. She wore a pink silk blouse that complemented her olive tint. Black slacks contained her butt. The double camping mattress in the sleeping cove wasn't so tidy. Luckily I had opened windows. Luckily we hadn't been in a hurry to go out to dinner.

"Rita, this is Judy, Judy . . . Bel's mom." My pathetic attempt to relieve tension—why should there be tension?—cut two ways. Citing Judy as an old friend probably didn't go over well with her; anything and everything about the situation probably irked Rita. After more of my awkward sounds, the two women found a common reference: the University, Judy for a BA, Rita for one rung higher. Inquiries were and observations were traded, but neither graduate pressed for revealing years.

Rita, who never stayed long on the drop-off, managed a "nice meeting you." "Yes, and the same," Judy replied. "I've always thought that Bel must have a very good mother." Did that "always" touch a nerve? did the familiar "Bel" feel threatening? The fragile peace between Belinda's parents had suffered a set-back.

"Your dad was telling me about that little boy in the park."
"Ah, what boy?"
"The boy in the park that you tried to help." I guess to a five-year old an incident two weeks ago was just filed "to forget." We'd been at the park across from the Rose Garden when this little fellow managed to hurt himself in the sand-box. Bel leaned over him with endearing tenderness and asked him what was wrong. The little brat, who I think was suffering more of a tantrum than an injury, flailed his arms at Bel

and kept on a whining cry. Bel persisted and asked, "Is your mother
here? should we get your mother?" Then from some lair a harridan
appeared, looked at us as if . . . and snatched the kid away.

"Oh, ya, I was just trying to help him."
Judy, her brown eyes softly caressing, held out her arms for Bel.
"That was very sweet, honey, very sweet. It was motherly and . . . very
conscientious. Is that too big a word for you?"
"I don't know. It sounds good."

About a year later Judy dropped in just for a minute to drop off a
windfall of books that she had scored from some growing-up kid's
mother. Bel accepted the goods with discriminating curiosity and a
hug. We'd been playing Spanish-style partnership dominoes, grown-ups v kids, me and
Ray v Bel and Josh. Josh, a latte-colored kid about Bel's age was one of
those above average kids and a game-playing whiz. Judy was
intrigued, she hadn't played in years and with a slight suggestion she
sat in for me. She scanned the dots that matched and branched; she
took the measure of her partner and their precocious opponents. I
hovered, lending a supporting hand to a shoulder or two and then
played host and mixed the drinks. I rinsed five varied glasses and
—no measure involved—served to great satisfaction a huge
smoothie of bananas, frozen raspberries, chocolate, cream, frozen
orange juice, soy milk and vanilla.

Sometime later we were at Judy's for a festive lunch of potato latkes
and apple sauce. Then Judy and Bel did a "just us girls" dress-up.
Seems Judy had a closet of retro or vintage or just old clothes. Her
full-throated laughter mixed with Bel's giggles. I just observed and

wondered at that playful enchantmen,: this child-like delight in
transformation: the kid trying on the raiment of the grown-up; the
grown-up indulging her kid-self.

Bel did a pirouette on her spindly legs, she was capped by
a feathered creation and her flowered house-dress came down to her
toes. "What do you think, Daddy?"
"Just adorable, honey, just absotively adorable."
"Oh, Daddy," she protested, "me and Judy think it's cool." Then she
selected a baby-blue fedora, jumped up on a chair and planted it
firmly on my head. "Now you can be in our movie."
"Movie?"
"You said we looked like an old movie," Bel said.
"Only in color," Judy added.

"I don't want to be a party-pooper girls, but we gotta go." Bel gave
only a twitch of her mouth, but her animation subsided. "Weren't
those the best latkes that you ever tasted?" I asked.
"Those were the only lakkies I ever had and they were yummy."
I looked at Judy, her brown eyes were beaming, I was beaming, we
were all on high beam.
"How about going to the bathroom," I instructed Bel, "and wash that
expensive looking stuff off'n your natural-born face." She stuck out
her lower lip in a make-believe pout.

In the car she said, "I like Judy." Kids, they say the darndest things.
"And you can tell Judy likes you, right?"
"Ya," she seemed to mull that and said, "And Judy likes you." We'd
been lovers, not very good for each other lovers, but as sometimes

happens we stayed, or perhaps, became friends. It was obvious,
however, that Bel was the linch-pin of that platonic pairing.

"How many people," I asked, "have all the *Wizard of Oz* books, by
which I meant all the L Frank Baum books. Judy sometimes read—
her timbre changing for each character—to her audience of two: one
more engaged, the other more admiring.

Bel laughed, "She's such a big kid."
"I'll tell her that, that's very nice to say."
"Daddy, don't."
"OK, but that's very nice to be—when you want to be—when
you're thirty-five or forty."
"Thirty-forty, that's older than Mama," Bel commented. And, I
thought, younger than Mama.

We reached the Altamont Pass and watched the windmills fly by. Bel
contemplated the familiar towers and asked, "How can you believe
in Big Foot and not in God?" "Because it's fun to believe in Big Foot,"
was the best that I could do. Rita and I had talked about a variety of
subjects and I assumed from the tenor of some of these that we were
both non-evangelizing atheists or agnostics. I don't remember talking
specifically about either of those Big Guys. I didn't think until years later:
why that question?

Those Sunday drives to Modesto always included something of a free
association dialogue. Bel was a conversationalist. She was a talker
since she had learned how. Just talk, amusing as that was, soon
became coherent communication. Then Bel, at about five, with seeming

spontaneity, could read. Bel demonstrated that magic, with that kid-like lovely combination of pride and modesty, one evening at the drop-off. It was one of those times that lights up your mind and lightens your heart. Bel hesitated at some pronunciations, but Rita and I could see the sparks of her mind. It was one of those times that we were of the same mind: the same generously loving mind. Why couldn't there have been more of that?

Chapter 19

"Lila and her brother Jamie lived on a ranch in Colorado. This
was way back about 1900 before cars. She was ten, Jamie six. They
liked to walk up into the hilly woods and pick blueberries. You ever
tasted real wild blue-berries?" "Nope," Belinda answered, "but
remember those juzzy razzberries we found in the park?"
"Oh, ya, weren't those tasty?"

"Lila told her mother where they were going and their mother said . . .
what do mothers always say?"
"Be careful."
"Yup, and in those days in wild Colorado there were a lot of wild
things to be careful about."
"Snakes?"
"Ya, rattlesnakes, cougars, lots of dangerous critters. But it was so

pretty up in the hills where you could see for miles; and there were
wild flowers, blue bells, columbine, poppies, all kinds of flowers."
She and Jamie would pick a bunch for their mother."

Once upon a time, a very long time ago, instead of reading a bed-time
story, I, making it up as I went along, told something of an adventure
story. From then on only a "real" story would do.

"Jamie brought along his jack-knife. In those days boys always had a
jack-knife."
"Why?"
"Um . . . they just did. Men carried guns, boys, carried a knife."
"What about the girls?"
"I don't know. I'm sure that some girls had a jack-knife. But Lila, she
just had a stick that she swished through the high grass to scare any
snakes away. Rattlers aren't out to get you; they just don't like to be
surprised.

They found some berry bushes. Lila said, 'holy cow, look at all those
huckle-berries, we should have brought two buckets.' 'Maybe three,'
said Jamie and proceeded to pick and pop—into his mouth. 'Blue-
berries,' he said. Lila didn't contradict him, now-a-days she might've
said 'what ever.' They were both crushing the *blue* berries against the
top of their mouths and running the blue sweetness all around their
getting-blue-mouths when Lila stopped, became real still and said,
'Shushh, be real quiet.' Jamie looked up wide eyed because his sister
sounded real serious."
"Now who else likes berries?"
"Bears?"

"Yup, and Lila saw two black bear cubs. Now if you see cubs, who else is going to be around?"

"The mother."

"Yup, and you don't want to be between a mother bear and her cubs."

"'There's a bear around here and one thing you sure don't want to do is run away,' Lila told Jamie."

"'You don't?' Jamie gulped."

"'Let's just stand real still until we can see where the mother is,' Lila whispered."

"'OK,' said Jamie silently."

"'They say if a black bear attacks, it's best if you play dead. And even if it bites, no crying.'"

"Jamie didn't want to say it, but he did,' I'm almost crying already.'"

"When they saw the bear it was on the far side of the cubs, so they weren't in between. But it stood on her hind legs and smelled the air. Then she got down and started toward them. Not fast, but straight toward them from maybe two hundred feet away. 'I got an idea,' Lila said and she took off her jacket. She stooped down and told Jamie to get up on her shoulders. Now take the jacket and hold it over your head; see, we're a big animal.'"

"'We are?'"

"'That's what the bear is going to think . . . I hope. Now let's yell real loud, but not like we're scared.' It took Jamie a minute to get his volume up, but they got a pretty good caterwalling going on. The black bear stopped, looked confused and turned around."

"Cater what . . . what's that?"

"Um, that's um, just yelling, maybe like a screeching cat."

"Dad?" Bel didn't raise up from her pillow, she just lazily inquired, "is

that really a real word." Her night-time companion with yarn hair and
blue button eyes lay there just as lazily, but didn't say a word.

"Um, I think so, but if it wasn't it is now." I didn't want to get all
lexical—it was time to go to sleep—so I got on with wrapping up.

"When they got home they were shaking and ran to their mother for
a hug. 'Me and Jamie scared a bear away,' Lila said and she sounded
pretty proud of it. Mother patted their heads and said, 'That's nice, dear.' But they didn't
have any flowers; they didn't pick any blue bells or columbines; that's the thanklessness
flower."

"The what?" Bel asked.

"Um . . . certain flowers are supposed to stand for something, to mean something, like a
daisy means something but columbine is the only one that I remember."

"Why does it mean that?"

"I don't know, honey, some things just mean some thing that I have no idea of."

Sometimes I'd do a super-condensed standard. Pip on the moors became "Piper." Hamlet
was stripped to a ghost story. And I seem to recall there was some getting even with
Claudius, but with much less blood-letting than standard productions. Hamlet and cast
usually dredge up something. Even your gorge—what ever that is—rising at that
graveyard recounting of—how many?—of those kisses.

Sometimes it would be something like the "kids in bear country"
adventure. The hero would always be a girl a little older than Bel. The
sub-text, it seems, wasn't so solidly integrated into Bel's appreciation
of the literary. What sort of tactics were used to void those didactic
exercises? What stories about the ogre could elicit the response that Bel was
"afraid" of her dad? And, then, much worse. Being under the control
of an insecure mother who may have thought she was being stepped

over in an imagined competition for affection, can, I guess, produce a "Stockholm" effect on the most mind-of-her-own kid. When Bel told me that she wanted to live with me and not her mother, I can only assume that that sentiment was told to Rita: either matter-of-factly as to me, or, perhaps, in anger. Where are Bel's memories of all that?

Where was my Jake to discern, in the not-so-hazy distance and closing in, the clumsy arm of the law?

Chapter 20

"The thing that's important to know is that you never know."
Diane Arbus

She looked quizzically at the baby seat in the back of my car. The sheen of her eye was teasing, her smile bemused. "So . . . ?"

"Cathy," I'd called out tentatively—it had been what? so long go. I thought I had recognized her movement as she parked groceries in a nondescript econo-box. She turned to see—had she recognized my voice?—and then called, "Jeff"? We crossed the parking while mutually, I imagine, assessing the change in the oh-so-familiar. We met in an almost-collision for a good-to-feel-you-again hug.

Such situations are sometimes awkward, but we felt no test, no trying us for such an acute meet. We were both composed enough to not do the "so what have you been up to" routine. But the car seat—actually Bel had graduated from it some time ago—required an explanation. I was happy, even proud to explain, "That belongs to Belinda." "You have a daughter?" she exclaimed as a question.

"And I'd like you to meet her, I enthused presumptuously."

"Sure," she said, "sometime . . . soon."

*"This land is your land, this land is my land . . . from California to the
New York island."* You know the words, Belinda, help me out. Bel—
the things they learn in day care—did, indeed, know the words.
*"From the redwood forest to the Gulf Stream water, this land was
meant for you and me."*

Now Belinda had, if not three mamas, three maternal influences.
One read to her, one talked *at* her, and now one that sang with her.
Back in Modesto Bel's mother had the responsibility to get her to
day-care, then school, then soccer and all those good-for-kids
activities. At my place, on the week-end, there was no bothersome
hurry-up, there were stories, games, conversation and now singing.
And trips: Bodie, The Headlands, Pinnacles, or just on the way
to Modesto where we'd stop at the Oakland Zoo and visit a handsome
and expressive guy, the howler monkey. Among other hikes we did
Mount Lassen off-trail in the snow and then slid down the steep side
using my jacket as a sled. I think it was the Yolanda Trail on Mount
Tam where we found where the red-wing blackbirds flock together.

In retrospect it was cruel; it was burdening a child with more conflict
and dissonance than any kid could handle. Should I have known that?
What should I have done? been more stand-offish and authoritarian?
There was discipline, but withholding of affection was not part of it.
Perversely, I was accused of being too "cold" and treating Bel as a "peer."

When Cathy—with much welcome—became a sometime visitor,
and Bel and I were once-in-a-while visitors with Judy, it made for

friendships of a rather unconventional sort. Cathy—she had other interests—and I didn't take off where we'd left off, so I had then, friendships with two ex-lovers. Bel had friendships with two adults who regarded her not as if she were just a kid on the fringe, not as the center of *all* attention, but as a person of interest and respect. How much did Rita know about about those "just friends" relationships? Such unorthodoxy probably would've been cited as evidence of my perversity.

"What should we sing next?" Cathy asked. Bel did amuse herself with little sing-songs, but I'd assumed she resembled her parents in that art and her talents lie elsewhere. But she was at least as musical as I was; while driving and listening to the radio, I'd ask, "What instrument is that? Hear that mournful cello?
Mournful? That means sad, sad in the way . . . . the way . . . like when you lose someone."
"You mean like when someone dies?"
"Well, yes, that's one way . . . ."

I remember her keeping the beat with Jerry Lee Lewis and, much differently, she became perhaps the youngest fan of the indescribable Laurie Anderson.

Bel answered, "All the pretty little horses."
"Let's see if I remember . . . *Hush little baby, don't you cry.*" And that duo sang, to my surprise, I knew nothing of it, that . . . well, odd and pretty little song. "*. . . when you wake, you'll have a cake and all the pretty little horses.*" Well Bel hadn't been a baby for some time and not yet wanting a horse, but we had a nice little hootenanny and then called for a pepperoni pizza.

"Night cap?" I held up a glass in each hand and Cathy pointed to the
bottom book shelf where the bottles (an earth quake precaution)
were. Her hair was shorter, all the better to expose her elegant neck.
The fine lines had a start, but the soft-light of her blue eyes was as alive as
I remembered that radiance. As effortlessly as a dancer, she folded her legs
beneath her and settled on the rug as lithely as a teen-ager. It was just
the imagining of a memory, but the sight of her slight exposure
seemed to elicit, for an ephemeral blink-of-the-eye, the scent of her:
her salt-sea primal smell. I poured two Bristol Creams.

I don't know her, do I," she asked.
I took a sip of the sweet wine and sighed, "No, but I really don't
either."
"So your status is . . . divorced?"
I laughed ruefully, "No, not married. We weren't close enough to
have such a conflict."

That was years after the Adriana non-affair and after a reconciliation
of sorts there had been, necessarily, some closeness and, to my mind,
still some unnecessary conflict. But I didn't want to inflict gossipy
truths on our new friend. To change the subject, I asked, "What's with
Zach these days, I haven't him since . . . oh, I don't know."
Cathy grimaced to report that, "He's in L A."
"Let me guess, he got an offer he couldn't refuse and like Holden's
older brother he's . . . ."
"He's dying."
"Dying?"
"AIDS."

Chapter 21

"No rules, however wise, are a substitute for affection and tact."
Bertrand Russell (on education and discipline)

"Dear Ants." That's how Belinda started a thank-you note to my aunts Alma and Edna, who would be her great aunts, or, maybe unofficial great aunts. "That's the common-sensical way to spell aunt," I explained, "but for some reason, I guess it was a French word and some still pronounce it *aunt*. You say toe-*may*-tow and I say toe-*mah*-tow, that sort of thing." Bel was not impressed with my lesson, but I ploughed on. "How do you pronounce this?" and I wrote "right."

Sensing a good-natured trap, she said, "rite."
I said, "right you are." Then I spelled "rough." "How about that?"
"That's ruff."
"Right, but how do you know when the 'g h' is like an 'f' and is sometimes silent?"
Bel laughed as if to indicate, OK, dad, you're a tease but I'll go along with it.

"How the heck do you know how to speak English so good?" I asked.

Are first-graders even aware that they speak English?

"I don't know, I just do."

"Well, English is a nonsensical language and I think it's a supercalifrigeous achievement that you speak it like a good American should."

"Daddy," she came back with mock irritation, "all the kids speak English."

"Really," I widened my eyes in surprise, "that's very impressive. How about the kids that speak Spanish?"

"Mama can talk Spanish."

"I wish I could do that, Spanish, Arabic, Italian . . . I'd sure like to speak Italian, but . . . does mama talk any Spanish with you?"

"I know what gracias means."

"That's a good word."

"We say it at school like when we get our crappy lunch."

"But getting back to your letter . . . did mama suggest that you write?"

"She said it was nice to do."

"It is nice to thank them for the Christmas present—that thingamajig—but . . ."

"It broke."

"Broke?"

"It musta got wound up too tight," she explained.

"Well, things come and things go, but it's the thought that counts."

"The ballerina wouldn't go, she wouldn't dance without the music."

"Well, anyway, it was very thoughty of the aunts to send you a lovely present and it's very thoughty of you to thank them, but it was really a 'gift' because to get a present you have to be . . . ?" Bel adjusted her beret to better ensnare some blond hair and shrugged.

"When you're in school, you are . . . ?"

104

Perturbed at such nonsense, she did a sarcastic "prez zent."
"Right, everybody says present but when everybody is wrong they're
right; does that make sense or not?"
Bel just rolled her eyes and wagged her head; the comic confusion
had played its self out. She said, "Let's play UNO."

Years later a Google search revealed that she'd done some writing:
a few restaurant reviews in a college paper. She always did have a
rather adult discrimination about food. She returned, for instance,
from a posh wedding reception with her mother and the observation,
"Ooh, the smoked salmon."

She was also a precocious observer of the real world. I remember
watching a documentary while Bel, on the floor beside me
entertained herself with a couple of Barbies. (I wasn't a Barbie fan; Rita
was anti-Barbie; they were presents from Judy.) When she glanced
at the screen, I asked, "What war do you think that is?"
She watched for a minute and said, "World war two?"

Perhaps WW1 and WW2 were the only wars she'd ever heard of and
her answer, Jeopardy-like, was a good guess. But I'd contrast that
first-graders answer with a question that I'd just read about: a USC
coed of Chinese descent asked in a discussion about such, "Oh, did
we fight Japan in world war two?"

Bel had some answers and she had more than her share of kid-like,
inquiring mind questions. She came to accept split housing but at
four or so she would wish that mom and dad lived together and why
not. Why did you get divorced was a tough one because, of course,
we didn't. Did she ever ask her mother such questions? Did she
ever tell her mother that she knew which war was which?

Chapter 22

"Convictions are more dangerous foes of truth than lies."
Nietzsche

After various indignities, including Rita's over-the-top speech at the sentencing. I
had at several obligations. One was a once-a-month meeting with a probation officer;
another was getting a "volunteer" job to do 500 hours of "community" service; the very
mandatory therapy with Dr Maye that was supposed to last for the five years of
probation, plus continued shelling-out for various billings.

Then there was the assumed obligation to Belinda and to the truth, which involved many
miles driving to Modesto to see Bel's latest therapist. A therapist, incidentally, who was
the business partner and the mentor of the principal therapist in the case. I soon realized
that those trips were just driving to a stacked deck. I never did see Bel. I gave up a lost
cause, sold the truck and moved across the Bay to a hotel in the Tenderloin.

One cost that a reluctant judge brought down—to not much over a hundred bucks per
—was child support. I had earned next-to-nothing for years. I did not have the health
to, and if I could, who the hell would . . . . ? It's tough enough getting a job with clean

clothes, a clean face, a somewhat cleaned-up work record and no "have you ever been arrested" to deal with. But I was looking for a no-pay job that I could do for an hour or two a day. I was, phone-call-getting late-charge deep into two credit cards. If that family court judge could've thrown me into debtor's prison, I inferred from his sarcasm that he would have done so with pleasure.

That a BAWAR-besieged judge and a hard-ass DA didn't sentence me to some lock-up, was—I have to admit—quite an accomplishment by Flynn. An imperious and irritating know-it-all, he got the job done. Not being sent to jail, say nothing of that growing enterprise known as the California State Prison System and the fact that I got off with "only" probation should have, I thought, got me off to a less-than-hostile start with my new overseer. Boy, was I wrong.

The officer's office was small; it was a squeeze-in closet with a gray metal desk to separate the professional from the con. My rather commanding officer was a small-minded, and conveniently small-framed woman. She featured beady dark eyes, a severe, bangs-down do, and an aggressive and a venomous attitude.

But, I'm being unfair. How is a probation officer, who deals—in probably tedious succession—with sociopaths, malevolent idiots and various sorts of conniving bastards going to greet her next client? Hello, Mr Hodges, I'm so glad to meet you; I'm Ms Bender and we'll be having these "getting-to-know-you" meeting for the next five years. Not likely.

She laid down the law; she stated her name emphatically as if the "bend" in Bender had some meaning. This was probation and keep out of trouble and fulfill your obligations or it's Santa Rita for you. Her wall paperings, beside the standard certificates, was a comprehensive collection of feminist propaganda. I'd seen it all before, a herstory of banners, signs and designs. Now, in the aggregate backing up an obvious true believer, the effect was menacing. But the imagination, when under stress, does tend to run amuk.

I made a variation of my disclaimer: "I say this only for the record, there is no reason for me to believe me, but I've committed no crime and I've certainly not harmed my daughter in any way." Bender glared, "Mr Hodges, you're a child molester. You're guilty of molestation and if you think you can blow smoke you might damn well find yourself on the Sheriff's bus to Santa Rita."

Oh, why couldn't they have left me alone to "homestead," to build, to stay clear of all the mad people? I was taken aback and pissed-off. After taking a minute to stay calm and expressionless, I said, "Well, after you're more familiar with the case you might have a different opinion." "Mr Hodges, your case is closed. We're not here to determine how guilty you are."

"Of course not," I agreed, "that's over. I was thinking not in the legal sense, but, I guess, in the ontological sense." For some reason she didn't seem at all amenable to entertaining my pretentious alternative.

She reiterated her reality check and put a date on an appointment slip.

Chapter 23

"Raising children is an art rather than a science."
Bruno Bettelheim

"Tantrums?"

"I think that was the critical . . . . the thing that put her over the edge.
But I sure had no idea when they started. I guess Bel—both of
them, actually—had had been in therapy for some time; therapy
that I didn't know about. Isn't that curious? Bel never mentioning
anybody, any other, a third party, any fourth party. What could have
been going on . . . ?"

"What? well, that, as you say, is curious, mighty curious," Dr Maye
added.

"It seems that Bel had these awful scenes after she came back after
week-ending with me"

Maye looked thoughtful and "Hmmm'd."

"I suppose to at least one of those therapists—I don't know how
many she was shopped to—that was just putting this-then-that

together; effect means a cause: ipso facto, bad dad." I paused while chunks of time fell into place as if they were scheduled. "But isn't it odd that this is before accusing me—blaming was standard procedure—that they're going to therapy that I don't know about, yet Rita is still taking the trouble of delivering Bel all the way to Berkeley most every Friday evening?"

Then those excruciating months, half a year? of only those few phone calls. Very painful for me and for Bel, but what was the nature of that pain. The primary punishment for Bel was that she couldn't see her dad. Her long distance "I'm sorry Daddy, I'm sorry" was crushing. Despair and helplessness were overwhelming me; I imagine it was about the same for Bel. No, I couldn't imagine and I feared what I couldn't know. I couldn't contain myself with memories and started to spill over. I needed some of the handy kleenex.

After giving me a minute Dr Maye asked, "Did you ever see Belinda have one of those terrible scenes?"
"No, I heard over the phone Rita having an hysterical fit. She, for instance, yelled, 'Do you hear that? I've locked her out to protect us both.' She'd go on-and-on about her 'stress' and having to correct my 'damage.'"
"Damage?"
"One was treating Bel as a 'peer.' Later she was 'afraid' of me."
"But she never acted any way like that with you?"

"She had only a few minor misbehaviors. I spanked her a couple of times. The last time it made so little impression on her that we had a little talk. I explained that she was too big to be spanked—my

112

'beatings' didn't faze her—and she should be good, not because she
might be punished, but because it was good to be good. Something
like that. I didn't get into the concept of the good life and ethics and
all such . . . . which, well, since it's over my head, was probably a little
advanced for a first-grader."

Once when Rita was still at my place from a drop-off, Bel, for some
reason got into an ugly pout. I knelt down to eye-level with her—I
wanted Rita to see how you deal with these matters—and talked
calmly and patiently with her. Within a few minutes we had the
matter resolved with a hug. I turned to Rita, she had left."

The telling of that left me, again, in an exhausted and defeated state.
You act in the most loving, tender and . . . *appreciative* way and you are
. . . the terrible and dangerous one.
"Ever see parents, "I asked, "who seem to have little appreciation of
their children; they don't regard them as . . . ."
"Yes, I've seen such. Sometimes in a family therapy situation, it's
easy . . . ."
"Bel was more of a 'project' to Rita than a real kid. She got her into
the best day-care, the best first-grade, that sort of thing. She was
probably already thinking SAT . . . entrance tactics. I will say, that during
her pregnancy she was very conscientious: no alcohol, no drugs not
that she was much of a user, and even her coffee, which, I'm sure,
took a lot of self-discipline."

Dr Maye, when I got into emotional mode tended to silence, pulling
at his lip while the wheels of his mind, processed, graded and cross-
referenced the incoming. After not too many sessions I could only

infer that he did that complex task conscientiously and as accurately as these memory-laden musings can be. He would cross one khakied leg over the other and, as if to keep thoughts from straying, press three fingers to his temple.

"Rita did have her form of affection; at her departure she would do a pro forma hug hug good-bye scene. Ya, the good-bye. Rita would call up from outside and, when Bel leaned out the window to wave, she'd call, 'Don't fall out.' If she'd seen us on our hikes and climbs she would've had a cow."

I went back to those times. How to preserve the purest memories when . . . . well, what has happened to them? What are those memories to Bel? How much of her has been . . . erased?"

"I also encouraged Bel to give her mother a hug when I brought her home. I remember, once especially, Rita positioned herself behind the table in an oddly defensive manner. Did you ever see that documentary about mothers who just don't have that maternal instinct?"
"No, but I think I know what you . . . what you've seen."
I just said, "I've got more maternal instinct than she's ever known."

Chapter 24

"A lie would have no sense unless the truth were
felt more dangerous."
Alfred Adler

"She seems an independent sort," Dr Maye surmised, "quite strong
minded."
I had to tug at my chin at that half-right observation: strong minded
or just fixed idea and rigidly minded. "So she seemed."
"But."
'She'd go to pieces at the smallest thing, really at nothing, something
that was really nothing."
"How so?"

How? Why? One incident came too readily to mind. Rita had dropped
Bel off at my place. After a minor tiff with Bel, as if threatened by some
sudden and severe realization, she stiffened defensively. Her full lips
contorted and she seemed to stifle a scream. I went to comfort her and
opened my arms. She ran past me and out the door. Belinda and I, both
stricken by that strange escape just looked dumbfounded at each other.

What could I say? I opened my arms to comfort Bel; and she me. In a half-apology, some time later, Rita did explain that the situation— what ever that was?—brought back some childhood trauma. "Stress" was mentioned. Why now this panic, this aversion? The woman had been in my arms many times, comfortably and passionately: why this?

"How so?" the Dr repeated, bringing me back to the here-and-now.
"Well, maybe the first indication was that Adriana non-affair."
"Before that, during her pregnancy, what . . . ?"
"I don't know. As the expression goes, I wasn't there for her."
"So, Jeff, you think this goes back to that: not being there for her?"
Of course it had. She carried the child; she carried resentment; she carried a weapon. The subject exhausted me. Was I feeling guilty?

"I was leaving her alone, she was leaving me alone." Should I be feeling guilty?
"No demand," Dr Maye asked, "for support, marriage . . . emotional support?"
"There were never any demands. Not any during her pregnancy. When Bel came on board I paid support. Later, among other lies, she said I didn't. I don't know which she valued most: the emotional pay-off or just a plain old pay-day?"

"It would seem," Maye observed, "that the transition from out of the picture to being a dad and paying support is confusingly unclear." Yes, it was true that I was so muddled about that critical time, that change-over time, that I really couldn't give much of an explanation or description. The memory: it both intrudes and deserts you.

Dr Maye switched gears and revisited another critical issue, "So, the
hold over you was . . . ?"

"That she would take Belinda away from me again."

"But there was a reconciliation?"

"Of a sorts, out of the blue. I didn't ask any questions, I was thankful."

"Why," the doctor smoothed his mustache as if making more room
for coherence, "why . . . do you have any idea? . . . why this change of
heart?"

I don't know how much heart was involved, but I conjectured, "Maybe
she just needed a week-end baby-sitter, which I was for, oh, maybe
more than six years."

"She needed her week-ends for . . . ah, socializing?"

"Quite the contrary; she was working on a dissertation, another degree?"

"What was that about, the dissertation?"

"I have no idea. She's—she's even used the expression to describe
herself—a do-what-it-takes woman. And, incidentally, Mrs Conseco
found out a bit about some very not-so-nice aspects to that trait of hers."
I paused to let Maye recollect and then said, "And I'm the sociopath."

I surveyed the cool, muted color room as if looking for something.

"I guess you know I took a lie-detector test?" He pursed his lips and
asked, "And?"

"I failed. Or it was, I guess, ambiguous, certainly nothing to show to
anyone. Flynn didn't want me to take it, I insisted."

"Let me guess, he had you take the test with a tech that he works with."

"Good guess?"

"Just standard procedure."

"But the thing is, I never saw the results. I paid for them, but like
much else I wasn't privy to them."

"So?"

"So I don't trust Flynn. At the time I was in such stupification that . . . .
I . . . didn't think . . ."

"You think . . . ?"

"I don't know. If I pass it doesn't change the case, but it might put
more of a . . ."

"It could have." I waited for Dr Maye to fill in that conjecture, "Flynn
talks to the judge, it sure wouldn't hurt to cite some inadmissible
evidence. It wasn't a trial."

I wish I'd had the good doctor on my defense team.

He added, "I guess that Mrs Conseco had the judge's ear. She went to
bat for you, must have."

I hadn't considered that. "Ya, you're right, she must have. And the
biggest factor in that was probably Rita."

"How so?"

"The deluge of letters to that PO, phone calls too, probably very
aggravating calls. It probably revealed to her an hysterical and
manipulative woman."

"Ya, you've described her as such before, but how so?"

"I've gone over this before. Ferinstance, her diagnosis of my father as
the molester of all his children."

"Not so?"

"Especially not so. And I was supposed to have $60,000 in the bank,
CDs I guess."

"Not so?"

"Half-so, or so . . . and I didn't talk about money, so how the hell did
she think she knew?"

"She wanted it?"

"For this, for that, she even had a list with amounts including a few
thou for BAWAR."

The doctor wrinkled his brow and repeated, "BAWAR?"

118

"At each hearing two or three of those women would be there. I wouldn't have known, but Flynn pointed, well he didn't point but he knew."

His fingers stroked his mustache again, "I've had some dealings with that outfit."

"And?"

"Their cause, their "war" is against rape, but, well, as sometimes happens a good cause becomes too ideologically rigid, the agenda too, well, just too much."

"Agenda," jogged my mind. I'd described therapists who, obviously, were "pro child" beyond any bounds of objectivity, as having a "a priori" agenda. There were cases of eliciting salacious accusations and, of course, the "repressed memory" phenomenon. And I wondered years too late: why those "we have to talk" meetings at cafes or the Student Union or some neutral and public place. "So," I asked, "would you indict some of your profession for having that same over-enthusiastic 'get daddy' agenda?"

"Agendum . . . and no, not an observation I'd make," he stated.

"About that polygraph, the odd thing was is the guy never asked me what I did or didn't do. He asked is Belinda lying when she says such-and-such. Is that standard procedure?"

"Hmmm, I'll have to ask someone."

"And then there was the Minnesota Multi test that Flynn had me take; what a crock of shit."

"The MCMI 11?"

"I guess. It cost 600 bucks to characterize me as the worst kind of pathetic scoundrel."

Maye cracked a slight smile and asked, "What did it say?"

"Well, it concluded with 'the patient is unlikely to reoffend.'"

"Anything else, anything specific come to mind?"

"My mind, I guess, can't record such gobbledygook. And, again, I don't have a copy of this . . . pseudoscience bull shit."

"I wouldn't call it that."

"What would you call something that compares an individual with convicts from Louisiana and Minnesota or where ever . . . on the basis of such questions as 'do you believe in god' and 'have you ever had a rash on your stomach.' Do you know what Senator Ervin said about such 'personality' tests?"

"The Watergate guy?"

"Ya, his committee on such. I think 'balderdash' would sum it up."

"I'd say it's valid if its administered correctly."

"Really? If I or anybody made invidious characterizations about an individual based on any group, he'd be guilty of 'stereotyping.' Isn't that the case?"

"Actually," he said through a pained smile, "it's pretty damn accurate."

I couldn't come up with anything that challenged his confidence in such common-sense-denying orthodoxy, so I weakly deferred, "It may make generally accurate predictions about a group but not an individual."

"Maybe you should take it again; maybe if it was done right . . ." I frowned quizzically, "You do that test?" I exaggerated the frown when he answered in the affirmative. "One finding that I do remember was that I was an irresponsible vagabond that moved around too much to be normal. I'd been at the same job and only several addresses for almost a decade, well, until I went north. I

went to build a house. How decadent and irresponsible is that?
Well, some would say it's a little unrealistic to quit a job to put
yourself in a very iffy situation, but isn't that like something made
to order for a defense attorney?

Dr Maye shot his blue cuffs through his tweed sleeves and then
kneaded the back of his football-player neck. "Sounds, again, like
you don't exactly trust Flynn."
"Exactly, but I don't have anything more to do with him."
"I'll give him a call and see if he'll release that test."
"You can do that?"
"I can try."

But what, I thought, would be gained by access to that report? That
Dr Weber was either incompetent or provided only selective intel?
I'd made that psych a nut-case within five minutes of his
interrogation, but I didn't disclose that diagnosis to Dr Maye. Such
unequivocal assertions by anybody in my vulnerable and lowly status
would be suspect and probably symptomatic. To read that report, a
certifiable scientific report from an uncertified nut case: would that be
amusing or just dispiriting. It did, I admit, have a few accurate and
apt observations, but then so does the daily astrology report.

An enthusiast of the zodiacal science once told me: *Your refusal
to compromise can sometimes result in some lonely periods.
Being a pioneer often means a lonely path and your challenge
may have been to search long and hard for your ideal home.
Your determination to stubbornly maintain your self-reliance
has been your main strength.*

Chapter 25

*"The captive princess' real father is depicted as benevolent, but,
helpless to come to the aid of his lovely girl."*
Bruno Bettelheim

Dr Maye informed me that, "Mrs Conseco said that Rita was
preoccupied with her own abuse . . . . with her own wretched childhood."
That officer had been off the beat for a while, but the good Dr had
conscientiously gone back to investigate that past. To rely on a single
source, especially one on a figurative couch is—I would agree—
not the best way to get to the bottom of these things; though I imagine
that many of those situations are a bottomless pit.

Somebody throw me a rope, I thought at the time. I'm wasn't going
to hang myself; I can get out of that hole; well, maybe not
emotionally or financially whole, but more or less intact. But even
those on my "side," those who thought me certainly innocent, some
must have thought that short of doing the awful things that I was
accused of, I had to have done something; where there's smoke there's

fire. But I wasn't just innocent; I was more than simply the opposite of guilty. I couldn't, however, try to make that complex case; the truth would not be credible. It would sound much too self-justifying.

"She talked," I informed, "about some of that; she called it emotional abuse. Her step-mother . . . well, her father—he was a lawyer—just wasn't inclined to defend, to intervene . . . . that's the impression I got. And that high-powered lawyer had enough juice to get a trophy wife while his kids were still young."

"Is that how Rita described him? both of them?"
I tried to reconstitute those brief allusions, but it was old stuff and I probably wasn't too attentive at the time. "I don't recall much specifically, but dear step-mom was vain, attractive and mean as hell."
"Her biological mother?"
I blanked. She must've told me something of her mother. "I can't remember any mention . . ."
"That's odd, he gets the kids *and* a trade-up wife. I wonder what was going on there?"
"You'd think," I added, "that if step-ma was so abusive that Rita would express . . . express some yearning for her mother." We said nothing, as if thinking about what was so out of the ordinary, so odd.
"Maybe it was too painful to talk about," I offered so psychoanalytically-like.
We said nothing.

Then, for some reason leaving the mother-subject, I asked, "Have you ever read Bettelheim's 'Uses of Enchantment?'"
"Well, Bettelheim has been pretty much discredited," he responded.

"That's so, I guess, but it's very interesting . . . about fairy tales."

"Tell me about it," he said as if not especially interested.

"Very Freudian, seems that those stories, so he says, evolve . . . the parts
that . . . ah, resonate psychologically, they help kids resolve conflicts:
love, violence, hate, sex, dependency; those sorts of things, those are
the versions that last."

He cast me a quizzical look and said, "That's more or less what I
remember from a New York Review."

"But on the other hand," oh wasn't I the expert, "those Grimm guys
are just grim, they're dull, morbid and not exactly bed-time fare for
kids. And speaking of Freud, which side are you on in that
controversy?"

"Well, as you can tell, I'm not exactly a Freudian."

"Nor, thank god, a Jungian."

Dr Maye just grunted dismissively at that superficial opinion and then
said, "But speaking of the great man, the old Electra thing might be
relevant . . . in your situation." I just "hmmmed" and let him go on. "It
doesn't take that much for a little girl to have confusing love/hate
fantasies."

I wondered, as I had never dared before, just how knowing was Bel?
just how complicit was she? What resentments—or what caresses—
could have lead to this law, this very personal punishment?

"Especially," I added, "when she was encouraged to do so—much
more one than the other."

"Especially when her very existence—am I exaggerating here?—
is dependent upon someone with her own love/hate conflict . . . with you."

"Love?"

Maye gave me a "get up to speed" look. "You described your
relationship as . . . whatever it was, but primarily and simply sexual."

"And no romance," I concurred, "no sweet nothings, no implied
promises, and no . . ."

"No commitment, no exclusivity, no monogamy?"

"Ya, none of that."

"And she was satisfied with that?"

I shifted my uneasy weight—the weight of lingering guilt?—and
tried to think of something sensible, something justifying? "You know,"
I stretched for the sensible, "they say that most relationship problems,
all those bad marriage problems, are due to communication screw-ups."

"True, same could be said for problems in general."

"But, incidentally, I was accused of being 'uncommunicative."

"Why would she think that?"

"I don't know, I'm adequately verbal, Rita is too and not overly so,
but . . . we had trouble talking about problems that should have been
talked out."

"So you did have those common communication screw-ups."

"True, I'm having trouble explaining. what shouldn't be too
complicated. Even before Rita was pregnant . . . it was . . . the communication
was, well . . . was pretty superficial. No, I take that back, we *talked,* let's just
say it was less than profound, less than psychologically penetrating. It
was ordinary people having ordinary talk while we talked around what
should have been talked about."

"Let me guess, you two were locked into sexual dependency."

"Now you want to know about my sex life, isn't that a little intrusive?"
I said, trying to humor us out of this penetrating dialogue.

What I didn't want to get into were my ideas, well not so much ideas as reflexive—but somehow informed—responses; responses to the aesthetics of looks of course, and the breadth and depth of emotion and expression. I didn't want to sound like some wine snob; I didn't want to be one of those "sensitive" guys who talk—as supposedly opposed to bragging—about their relationships; and I didn't want to sound like those "connoisseurs" of women who has "types" and derogatory characterizations of those who do not meet his criteria. I guess I have some preferences, who doesn't? I'd also guess, however, that the qualities and style that one prefers is not found by looking, but usually occurs by fortuitous discovery: a sometimes simultaneous, sometimes deferred discovery about the other and within one's self. I have in some cases only after-the-fact regret. Certainly in this case regret came about slowly and then, in my too-slow realization that I was, with accelerating severity, not just an adversary but by the luck of some deterministic draw, a kind of prey.

"That sort of thing does come up in therapy."
"Oh, ya, getting to your point; I imagine that sex, be it good, bad or indifferent, does pass for love, maybe as often as not."
"That's a 'profound' generality, but . . ."
"OK, what I was dependent on, or maybe it was more of an ego-boosting . . . well, OK, dependency."
"How so, ego?"

I studied the potted greenery: ficus? aspidistra? I observed for the nth time the print with the floating tomato-red horizon. "Well, we were sexually compatible in a more than superficial way, and . . ."
"OK, with your libido, you mentioned your ego."

"Ah, yes, I guess that organ became inflated because I seemed to be . . .
ah, the instrument of her remarkable response . . ."

"Hmm, I see."

"You do? I don't know if I'm bragging or complaining."

The clock was running out. In a last minute evasion I mentioned that
I was going to have a PSA. At the VA.

"Just precautionary, no pisher problems?"

"Ya, just a standard my-age-you-do-it thing."

Chapter 26

*"The big difference between sex for money and sex for free
usually costs a lot less."*
Brendan Behan

"Most men don't know how to physically fuck, to say nothing of
making love," she had told me, I guess in appreciation after we had
done one somewhat more than the other. She should know; she was
in the business. It was cash on the night-table before she would
recline to play her part, before I could part her. "No wonder their
wives don't want to fuck them," was among the interesting
observations offered during a brief *tete a tete.* I hadn't done
anything exceptional except, perhaps, asking if she wanted to cum.

"Are you bragging or complaining?" Maye asked, as if reading my
mind, but actually in response to a less charged introductory remark.
"Just reporting, sir, it's my job."
"I hope you don't find the hours too onerous."

"Better than my daily gig of sweeping, mopping, wiping, waxing and all that various food business stuff."

"For?"

"For absolute zero, for nothing, but I confess there is some gratification. I'm getting in two hours a day, five days, so I'm almost half done. I'm really lucky not to have a real job, yup, really real lucky. I heard this at my lucky job and I'll only repeat it just this one time: we work at 'Lunch for Losers.'"

At that I went into mulling mood and stared at the steeple across the street. I had an interest in the architecture of small churches, small town churches—I should do a photo essay on such someday—but that awkward conglomeration of various materials—brick here, clapboard there, plastic-looking windows—was not one of those nor was it one of the notable churches in Berkeley.

"You know, when we do attend to the relationships in this case, but what was previous to this . . . this terrible fiasco, was pretty misleading. That telling, those women, girls . . . was quite selective. A few women, a few extra-ordinary women but the high-lights don't reveal the whole game. I think you're supposed to say 'sounds pretty ordinary to me.'"

"Check."

"Yes, simply misleading: I didn't . . . don't . . . want to misrepresent a life. There was, well . . . Cathy, and I did live with Francie for, oh, a while, and Gina from Sonoma, and so-and-so's ex—and Veronique, and a what was her name?' etcetera and a few more etceteras and did I mention . . . ? ah, yes, *Vair-on-eek*. All true if slightly embellished, but in between . . . way too many, way too long . . . ah, dry spells."

He shifted his big frame as if to brace himself for . . . a serving of self-indulgent pity or in readiness for therapy-appropriate revelations?
Well, all the same thing maybe.

"And Rita," he reminded me and then asked, "Francie?"
"Ya, well . . . that's a whole 'nother story. I guess I was just aimlessly going . . . wasting time. Where I was going I never . . .
do you remember a novel 'Boys and Girls Together'? . . . No, before your time I guess, but I was never in a boys and girls together situation. You know, like going to college, working in an office, not working swing-shift at the box factory.
"You did go to high school."
"Ya, don't remind me."

Dr Maye just waited me out. He didn't even do a thoughtful stroke of the mustache. He knew he'd hit a sore spot and I knew I didn't want to indulge in any more feeling sorry for myself. "I guess . . . yes, I guess it was women, not anything serial or there for the taking and making, but some good sex and companionship tends to make a feller a lot less aimless, maybe not some hankwilliams sorta guy, but I'm not . . .
Thing is that loner role plays well but in reality it's no *Picnic*, whether you're in some Salina, Kansas or walking down Broadway, not, I guess . . ."

"So it was sex that brought an end to that . . . aimlessness?"
"Only in retrospect do I see a change, there was no epiphany, no eye-opening experience. Maybe it was just staying in one town; not exactly settling down but not goin' down the line. You know I never hopped a freight. I got rides in various including maybe a Cessna single engine. I was an over-night guest in a freight car once, but all

131

that was, as I say, another life, but something of it, those memories
—for better or worse—still linger, still have influence." It occurred
to me that I was blabbering. I didn't want to go back, especially not
to go back to the start of that life when I packed my bag and split . . . .
split off from some semblance of a society of people. I had no
congregation; not that I felt a part of one when I was part of one.

"So, is it over now . . . that . . . loneliness?"
"The thing is I never thought of myself as lonely. I certainly was but
I didn't think of myself . . . that way. Fact is I didn't think . . . very well, I
just responded, just reacted."
"So how did that change?"
"Well . . . I didn't read a book called 'Thinking for Dummies' or
anything self-helpy and granted, there seem to be some recent lapses in
looking out for myself. But compared to, say, back in high school,
back in those two dyseducational years, I'd say . . . ."
"There you go, bragging again."
"I take your point, but back . . . . in those days I thought paradoxically
that real men were silent and they said clever things."
"And you've learned?" He allowed himself a slight smirk but reverted
to the conscientious listener.

Why was I going back to high school when that was the last thing I
wanted to think about? "It's just like high school, meaning that banal
will get you by." I paused, and satisfied with that insight I revealed
on, "I went to a singles bar once." I let the loaded banality of that sink
in. He waited me out.

"They spoke another language."
"Which was?"

132

"Oh, something . . . ever watch "Friends?"

"Sure."

"Sure?" I raised an eye brow.

"What language did they speak by in high school?"

"Quite standard. I wasn't inhibited by a language barrier. Well, there
was a common vocabulary, but still. there was a barrier."

Dr Maye squeezed his forehead as if to indicate that this . . . this
aimlessness had gone far enough. "So you're telling me . . . what? that
you are, that you were, not anti-social, but a social mis-fit."

"I guess you could say that." I didn't, off the top of my head, have
anything better.

He tapped his pen and speculated, "Interestingly, all those
aforementioned women, those selectively mentioned women, they all
had, I'd guess, more than two years of high school. What's with that?"

I laughed, "Yes, much more, but now you're getting personal."

"Now Jeffrey, I hate to break it to you but therapy *is* personal."

"I appreciate . . . your humor, but let me think about it."

"No thinking allowed."

He was right. I thought too much. Not too well but what he meant
was that I wasn't getting into the therapeutic swing of spontaneously
expressing my feelings and all that. Although we had abandoned the
court's direction to "cure" me, I certainly had some areas that could
use some looking into. To do that I would have to be more "open."
Not that I didn't indulge in dumb and impulsive utterances, but I just
couldn't—or wouldn't—get into that deep digging revelatory spirit
of therapy. What, for instance, *what was with those two years?*

I knew only too well the *why* of it; even while seemingly out of mind, it was a constant and inhibiting influence. I'd written, I remember about that and I thought later: too much information. But then I was paying a man whose job was opening up such cans of worms. But at that point I thought: *what's the point?*

Chapter 27

"Children sweeten labors, but they make misfortunes more bitter."
Francis Bacon

"Tell me about this house," Dr Maye inquired. He probably was genuinely interested.

"I've got a closet of a room in a SRO hotel with an air vent view."

"You don't want to talk about the house?"

"That's the thing, there ain't no house; the property is sold; no way will there ever be . . ."

The beams, the long beams that would've extended, and then some, the width of the house: 4x4s that I could have, with a ladder, handled by myself.

Maye's office had become a once-a-week home away from home. Certainly sitting in his leather easy-chair had been a luxurious alternative to sitting on my sleeping bag in the back of that pickup, but even now, the difference between my digs at the Hubert and his spacious room was something like when I was a kid and noticed the difference between our adequate home and, the wealthy-seeming dining room at the McCauley's with its velvety matched chairs and dark wood cabinets with glass that guarded shiny and extra-clean what-nots.

Never the less, I was of two minds about the doctor's office—one rational and appreciative, one resentful and regressive. I surveyed the room as if looking for an escape. There were four prints on east wall; the association I made was Rothko: floating soft edged horizons of dusty blues, ashy greys, mustardy yellows, that tomato red. That painter had left a financial mess. Less newsworthy was the excessively bloody mess he left. I came across that description, reading not about the artist, but about the business of cleaning up messes: including the left-overs of murder and suicide. He, who incidentally has that chapel of serenity or what ever—in Houston?—dedicated solely for his canvases, for some reason chose to give blood: all he had all over the place.

"It's probably just as well; I was giving out a little just starting the project. It's been progressive since . . . . On the other hand it would have been so . . . just so nice looking out over miles of wild-almost-no-damn-people."

"Just like Lennie and George."

"Or like George and maybe a Lynnie, but no chickens, no rabbits, no cow, no rows of beans."

"Progressive? so how's the kitchen work working out?"

I sighed, "No lie, it's a bitch. But—and the boss, Carol, has been great—it's been better since I got out of the heat and just doing dining room duty. I think Carol realized she'd have a passed-out hospital case if . . ."

"Doesn't sound like fun, been to the Doctor lately?"

"I did get in at the VA, but they're not too interested in this . . . So, no, not for for a while. You hear these accounts of people going from one doctor to another: pointless."

"They have a 'it's all in your head' diagnosis?"

"Oh, they just don't want to be bothered if there isn't a specific regimen to follow. It may be all in the head in the sense that it's neurological, there is not much to go on. You know what one doctor told me? This very athletic-looking guy says, "Stop drinking, stop smoking and get more exercise."

"Sounds like expert advice," Maye chuckled. I smiled in appreciation of his *simpatico*. I didn't mention that I did have an appointment with a urologist.

"Speaking of what's in the head and this is one of the common symptoms, the damn brain drains memories, names, the sentence you've just read."

"That noticeable?"

"Been so for some time and don't say you're just getting old."

"Ya, that would be frustrating. Now that you mention it, you seen a little late on some words, common words."

"After I read the morning Chron, the cognition switch doesn't . . . instead of reading I'll have to write . . . seems easier."

"Good idea if you've got the ideas," The Dr didn't seem taken with my half-serious idea. How many clients has he had who thought they could, would, should write some damn thing like the history of their depression or some such indulgence?

"So you're working but not working. How do you manage, for instance, paying this high-priced therapist every week? Dr Maye was charging me a hundred which, I knew but neither of us mentioned, was fifty below his rate.

"Ants." I answered. "Well, I've been given, loaned, what ever, but you know how long a hundred bucks lasts. But it's my dad's sisters—both widowed, who've really chipped in."

The generation before me, except for my parents and the good aunts had all faded to a faint memory while I was a kid. TB, pneumonia, a young uncle gored by a bull, they'd all left early. For some of them the work that was supposed to, someday, relieve them of their virtuous burden, killed them without so much as a thank you. Now I was an undeserving beneficiary of all those labors. I said thank you. Well, "chipped in" was hardly accurate. They ponied up, not thousands but tens of. But, even with a trusted confidant, could I say so?

"They have been very generous, kept my head above water."

"You're lucky to have such . . . life guards."

"Sure am." I was going to say what would I do without them, but that would be too true. I don't know what the hell I would've done. Trying to get on SSI had been a futile ordeal. regular social security—measly as that would be—was some time in some hazy future.

"Alma, for instance, when we were kids, would drop off a bunch of "Saturday Evening Posts." Colliers, "Ladies Home Journals" . . . "Life," magazines like those. We'd all read something or other and then Mom would pass them along to the lady down the road. She or Edna, both, were always there . . . always there in one way or another."
"They took an interest, they were influential?"
"Very, as later they were with Bel."
"You visited?"
"Four, I'd guess four times. Bel had become an experienced flyer. We agreed, for instance, that airline chow was better than school lunch. But for Mom and Alex and his wife and their girls, they all lost Bel—not just me—and she lost them."

And I'm missing her by some immeasurable factor. Will time diminish the affective sight of her sleeping after (or, during) the bed-time story?

"So, you'd reconciled with your family?"
"Oh, sure, ages ago . . . when I got out of basic, which was before Vietnam, which is back in history some place."
"The prodigal son came home?"
"I never thought about it, but what does 'prodigal' mean?"
"Hmm," he ran a finger down his jaw-bone while searching maybe the-bible-story-in-his-mind for an answer, "reckless?" he guessed.

"About those girls, little girls, Rita actually wrote Alex and Barbara that, because Alex had been molested—that diagnosis of hers—they should be careful and not let the molested be the molester. They thought she was a little unbalanced: salaciously and malevolently nuts.

Chapter 28

"There is no such thing as justice—in or out of court."
Clarence Darrow

Of course I thought of killing her. (Of course I didn't "share" this
with any of my official or unofficial confidantes.) I wouldn't but
why not? I couldn't get away with it; who would the obvious
suspect be? I didn't have the energy, ingenuity or finances to be a
career fugitive. I'd have to kill myself; that didn't seem a viable
option. *I didn't deserve it.* But such thoughts were fleeting and I
never seriously wished for Rita's death—not in any way and
certainly not by my hand. The feelings are mixed, but, I've always
—and continue to—wish for a good life for Rita and not just for
Belinda's sake. I even take a bit of attenuated pride in her
accomplishments that an e-search reveals. But I never loved her,
never came close; we were never was really close. Such feelings
may be cold-hearted, but they are hardly out of the ordinary. Maybe
it was the cloud behind her gray-blue eyes that revealed more than
melancholy. That such soul-pain should diminish her is unfair: tragic,
but commonly unfair. I understand a little about that.

139

I don't think I saw her at all after those so-called counseling sessions. Except, of course, at court; she was a ways away cross-court when she scored that vile forensic speech. Was that the high-light of her avocation?

"Nobody believes her," Lawyer Flynn comforted me. The "nobody" being the judge, the DA (not an assistant) and a few other interested parties. Certainly not the roomful of spectators who were there (including, I'm sure, some from BAWAR) for or against other defendants. I held my head high and tried, with a stoic and rueful expression to convey that 'this woman is mad and out of her mind.'

I hadn't said much to her since the first family court hearing when I told her I was sorry she had to go through all this but how it came about I don't know. "I've never harmed Belinda in any way, I never would and I think you know that." She dismissed me with an aggravated look and turned away. The last time she probably addressed me as a peer worthy of consideration was a few years previous to that forerunner of the even more serious campaign.

But "nobody believes?" Did she actually believe the various and curiously escalating accusations against me? Could somebody really make a coldly impassioned speech in a full court room unless they believed it? Well, she perjured herself about financial and insurance facts; she'd been accusing me, since the imagined Adriana "affair" of various faults and inadequacies.

Who knows? Perhaps the real malevolence is the enthusiastic willingness to believe. "I have to believe my daughter," she said once.

Well, such "have to believe" statements can be an attempt to relieve dissonance; they are an attempt to arrange reality so that the self can survive a threat. Who knows the intensity of the threat that she felt?

How could she not realize that my love and affection for Belinda would preclude my hurting her in any way? She certainly should have realized that sex for me was not a matter of domination or a sinister seduction. How did the different aspects of intimacy become conflated in her mind? projection? manipulation? Maybe what started as fiction—the mother's or the daughter's?—became, as therapists, cops and lawyers became involved, necessary "facts."

But, for all that, as time dulled somewhat the emotional pain, real physical pain gained prominence. The cause of such affliction is unknown but some would, considering the circumstances for me at the onset, suspect a causal connection. I wouldn't bother to speculate about something so dubious. What was more disturbing, however, was that the nature of the emotional pain changed from the mutual loss that Bel and I suffered, to my concern about being found out, being labeled as the worst of the worst. It was, again, another thing that I couldn't talk about; except, of course, in Dr Maye's office.

Did I think of killing myself? Of course, who hasn't? Well, not everybody and many who do do so in a vague or hypothetical way. They say that suicide is the act of turning anger against the self. It would seem that some of those acts are "objective" and have nothing to do with hostility; or, for that matter—what is the matter?—the assumed depression. Or is that pseudo-profundity not the case? A Alvarez, whose "The Savage God" I read years ago, says suicide is a "confession of failure."

141

I don't think that's the case; it can be, sometimes, quite the opposite. I've known two, plus a half-dozen attemptees. One of the former, a writer of little success did it the right way: a .45 to the temple. The other, the town's all purpose handy man, committed that mortal sin with a shot-gun.

I don't have a gun. As a convicted felon I couldn't legally buy one. Was that a bluff when I told Mrs Conseco that I wasn't going to any lock-up? I couldn't say. It would've taken a more oppressive reality to put me to the test. What I do know that I don't want to punish myself with needless pain. (I've had enough . . .) Do those, for instance, who walk into the Thames with rocks in their pockets have any idea of the physiologyical process involved? I wouldn't want to make a mess and I would not do the unoriginal jump off the Golden Gate Bridge. But all that is just speculative and just the natural musings of one snared by some bitch-godess of Fate.

Dr Maye once brought up the subject of forgiveness. I pondered that opening and considered it a relevant and natural line of inquiry. Would the S distance himself, bite hook-line-and-sinker or do verbal gymnastics to not get involved in a moral question?

"I don't think I could forgive Bel; she's not Bel; she's a teenoid mall rat."
"Mall rat?"
"Well, that's harsh, but the point is . . ."
"After what she's been through?"

The pain registered on my face but it reached much deeper. Why this uninformed characterization? I had no idea of what her life was like.

142

Well, maybe as I both desired and feared was that her behavior had, since not seeing or even talking with her dad, improved. My loss was keen and piercing; perhaps hers, by necessity and not volition, was a process of diminishment and dismissal.

"What's central here is that I can't communicate with her and she, it seems, doesn't want to—or maybe she's still that much under her mother's thumb. Years ago no visits, then no phone calls—that was the start, or maybe the mid-point—of a deliberate estrangement process. What would've happened if I'd just given up? Given up trying to see her, to protect her, to be her Dad? Did I know what I was risking by getting that family lawyer, trying . . . for years? Until I gave up."

I leaned back, exhausted, and closed my eyes to that open vein of . . . what? emotional over-statement? self-destructive truth-telling? "Do I forgive her, as they say, "in my heart"? It seems any forgiveness involves something more than brokering a deal between disparate parts of one's mind. What goes on in her heart?"
Dr Maye frowned and scratched his head. Was this, he may have asked himself, an embittered patient closing down or was this hostility an opening?

He asked, "What about her mother?"
I thought . . . and thought. I really didn't know what to think. Obviously there'd been hate there, "killing" and all that, but that had subsided. Not that there was any forgiveness, but I realized that in her paranoid and abuse-addled mind, she thought she was losing her daughter; which, through no fault of mine, she was. Bel telling me—and

probably Rita—that she wanted to live with me, may have pushed her past antipathy to desperate action. Understandable if not forgivable.

I could only say, "I don't know, it's confusing. For some reason I seem to be blaming Bel almost as much as Rita." I don't know what he thought of this new line of confusion, but that's his job: winnowing coherence from confusion, digging in the niches and crannies of the psyche.

But our relationship, therapeutically, was rather superficial; which, as I've indicated, was the way I wanted it to be. But because it was congenial and stimulating while also tactical, it was, in its entirety, the opposite of superficial. Then, of course, the best thing Dr Maye did for me was after about two years of the sentenced five, was convince Ms Bender that I didn't need therapy any longer. That was a life-saver; a hundred a week was killing me.

Chapter 29

"No matter how bad things get you go on living, even if it kills you."
Sholem Aleichem

"So what were you doing up north?" Bender had scaled back her
adversarial attitude. We weren't best buddies but after six of seven
monthlies, the visits weren't unpleasant. Since I was in San Francisco,
in the Tenderloin, it was an easy BART-under-the-bay to both the
P O's and Dr Maye's offices.

"I'd bought some land; I was going to build a house."
"A house, that sounds ambitious." What probably came to her mind
was maybe 2400 square feet of standard suburbabuild—.or, maybe,
a remote torture chamber.

What I had in mind was very unsurburban: no cooking stove, only a
hot-plate and toaster oven, a dorm-size fridge, catch-water for everything that didn't need bottled water, one sink for all washings, a wood
stove like the one I saw at a touristy visit to the light-house, and board

shelves instead of kitchen cabinets (usually ugly anyway, probably originally used to keep mice out (a cat to do that).

"Luckily I'd hardly got started. I didn't have a dog yet."

Her dark eyes pierced less ominously but she opened my folder; that generally meant some vexation from Rita.

Accusations of various non-payments were rebutted with canceled checks to the officer's satisfaction. Again, my adversary was, in effect and really inexplicably—she wasn't dumb—becoming my best witness.

"Rita tells me that Belinda is having emotional problems, some . . . . serious problems." Oh, god, of course: quite predictable. That Rita was still trying to influence the case was worrisome; for her have to pass on bad news was heart-rending. She seemed intent to keep on being my worst enemy. Who knows what was been going on in the Modesto house? The artsy and very nice house of a respectable high school teacher and the improbable member of a Methodist church.

"Rita, you can probably tell by now, *is* an emotional problem."

"She's been through an awful lot," Ms Bender replied, as if conceding some validity to my remark. Everybody, it seemed, had been through *an awful lot.*

"That's regrettable, but I won't say any more than that. The case, as you've said, is closed."

"She could be thinking civil."

If she was thinking, she'd know it wouldn't be worth the trouble. But, perhaps her primary motivation is to squeeze me emotionally. "She can't get blood out of a turnip," I responded sagely.

The wall of admonitions, slogans and exhortations, especially in that closet of an office, was still disconcerting. "Act Up," for instance, one banner told its captive audience. Who was supposed to "act up" and for what reason I don't remember.

"How's it going at the soup kitchen?"
It took me a month to find a "volunteer" job, or what? Santa Rita? It's quite understandable that non-profit organizations don't want a felon of my kind working for them—even for no salary. Just what is the point of sentencing felons to "community" service? rehabilitation? service that nobody else will do? Has anybody rethought this variation of convict labor? I thought I had done my last KP years ago, but there I was, dragging my ass through two hours of not-exactly-hard-labor. Luckily—again I count my blessings—I wasn't working so I could put in two hours a day at lunch time, and—oh, so doubly lucky—free lunch.

"I'm doing fine, have you talked to the boss, to Carol lately?"
"Last time she said you were doing fine." That was a very generous interpretation; she'd done me a favor getting me out of the kitchen; she knew I wasn't exactly fine.

"What drugs are you using?" Just like that, out of the blue.
"No drugs." Did I look like I was using? Of course most users don't look like some ratty-ass street addict.
"What drugs have you used?"
"I've had a few prescriptions and, of course, some marijuana in the old days."
"What prescriptions?" What got her on the drug theme? At least she

didn't have me roll my sleeves up. Maybe it's just standard procedure; maybe some client will be using and 'fess up. Then she could put a rule-breaking addict or a too casual user on that bus. I doubt that that line of inquiry was suggested by Rita. I wouldn't have been vulnerable to drug or alcohol accusations from her. Unless she flat-out lied, which she'd done . . . in how many instances? and how many that I knew nothing of and would never know?

"Oh, let's see . . . had a valium once.'
"What for?"
"Couldn't sleep."
"Guilty conscience?" She seemed quite satisfied with that insight."
I grimaced and scrapped fingernails across my teeth. "My conscience, then as now, is in pretty good shape."
"There's no law against self-delusion," she said icily.

Who the hell was she to make such pronouncements about me? It didn't bother at first, but all these people, everybody that I was involved with in this long drawn-out process, was *younger* than I was. I'm not going to figure it out but I must've been over a half-century and these damn kids had authority over me. They told me what to do, advised me what to do; all except Judge Silverstein who, luckily, didn't retire until after he'd handed down as good a deal as I could hope for.

I didn't volunteer that I'd used only a few pills, but ran out the prescription. I had a cache of those pink pills in their orange vials. Tranqs, which used to be handed out for the most minor aggravations were, as far as I knew, now difficult to obtain.

Her dark eyes both softened and narrowed; her brow creased as if to signify authentic concern. She paused and said, "You're going to get a big bill . . . and some bad news."

"What is it now? Has Rita outdone herself?"

"Belinda tried to kill herself."

I didn't, I couldn't respond. My mind went numb. Then a searing pain of an odd memory cut through that inert organ. It was all the more hurtful for being so joyous. The scene came to me, randomly I guess, of, after horse-back riding, an exciting first for Bel, we'd bellied up to the bar in a Columbia gold-country "saloon" for a real "sasparilla"; her eyes were alight from the thrill of the ride and I remembered those oh-so-happy blue eyes as we'd clinked our glasses: two compadres just off the dusty and danger-laden trail and having a cold one.

"She's OK. It was, from what I heard from the doctor, more of a gesture; one of those that wouldn't succeed but . . . well, it sounds as if she'll be in the hospital for a while."

Chapter 30

". . . but through it all I know that just to be alive is a grand thing."
Agatha Christie

I coped: well there were a variety of afflictions and aggravations,
but life was less a series of crises. One continuous bother was living
in the hellish St Hubert. Progressively hellish for the usual
demographic reasons. But I imagine the Hubert, with its clientele of
passive-aggressives, manic-depressives, alcoholics, users of speed
and crack and tough-guy ex-cons was probably how it is in the down-
scale life. Some, unlike myself, even worked for a living. But a call
from Seth said he had a lead on something that would sure as hell
put me up-scale a bit.

Morris and I were watching the Giants one evening when, with two
out in the ninth and the tying run on first and Matt Williams digging
in, there was a knock at the door.

We'd been, earlier, telling of misadventures and near-misses and I told of that huckfinnish find many years ago back in Hannibal. He didn't seem to appreciate what I thought was a very lucky—and very notable—coincidence. Well, some people just can't put two and two together to make a four that is more than minimally prosaic.

The knock was an unnecessary pounding—I wasn't in the attic, I wasn't in the basement—and it was ominous. Sure as hell it was the cops: two uniformed, one plain-clothed. They said I hadn't registered. I opened the sock drawer and took out my registration. My paper was in order. The cops left without comment. Morris pinched up his face in a concerned and inquiring squint and, quite understandably asked, "What the hell was that?"

I just took a cleansing swig of beer and asked casually, "You ever happen to get mixed up with the wrong, the very wrong woman?" He nodded as if he understood completely and then we heard the announcers' plaintive tone telling of the "what if's" that follow a loss.

Every year, just before my birthday, I had to go to the Hall of Justice and, always after an agonizing wait, do the ink-print, the front and profile photo mug shots and initial and sign a long list that says you do or don't do this-that-and-the-other, or you, the worst of the worst are going to jail. A few days later I'd pick up my mail at the front desk and it seemed as if the clerk would look at me for two seconds instead of the usual one. He knew, they all knew just what that envelope with that Bryant Street return address was.

That little paper makes one a pariah. I could move to Eureka or Crescent City or where ever, but that registration process anywhere but in a big city makes any sex-crimes registrant a marked man. Imaginations, as I guess Rita's did, just might indulge in the most fearful fantasies. So I was in San Francisco, among other more usual and desirable reasons, for anonymity. That and no car.

Housing in San Francisco is a bitch; and only the many homeless are of a somewhat lower status than those who live in SRO hotels. My closet of a place at the St Hubert featured a lone window that looked out at another window. Then there were the door-slammers, high-volume TVs, and most irritating, the music-lovers who shared their noise with innocent neighbors. The Patels had given up trying to keep the db level down.

When I called the cops on three Mexicans (in one room) it was made clear that I wasn't to do any law-enforcement. They didn't want any police calls to their hell-hole; and they, the Patels were most likely breaking the law. The Mexicans, who had a very different idea of "rights" than I did, didn't appreciate the cops either.

But to that new room; Seth called and told me to call a man who managed a shared flat deal in The Sunset. He'd talked with the accommodating guy and told him about me and said that every thing sounded copasetic. There were three windows with even something of a view, a hard-wood floor, and about three times the space that I was lucky to vacate.

I was yet one more time the man alone in his room, sentenced in a sense to some comfortable solitary and—for several reasons—inactive. But I wasn't monkishly contemplative; I was plugged in.

I had with phone and e-mail, some some-time conversationalists.
They varied, some for politics, one for just a 'what are you reading?'
another for what ever people talk about or just that contact that has
some meaning. None, however, for that memoir thing I mentioned a
while back. There was one conversationalist that I still missed.

And I missed people, in-the-flesh palpable people. I didn't miss
working but I did miss the brief exchanges I had at each stop.
Especially I miss Linda; she was at the Cypress Grove Rest
Home which was the last stop on the peninsula run. I looked
forward to having some time to kill when we made our
sign-over transaction; she would pop her dark eyes in mock
surprise at my welcomed intrusion. I missed that split-sec of an
alluring smile and then our brief interlude of small but mutually
fulfilling talk. Late in the swing shift her duty was light and, for
instance, a laid-aside Tony Hillerman could spur a condensed
conversation. Yes, I missed real people and I especially missed a
certain sort of responsive person . . .

My remote wouldn't quash the commercial, so when I answered the
phone that evening I couldn't hear all that clearly and she said, "You
don't recognize my voice, do you?" "Ahhh, no." What a shame; I
would always recognize that smooth, low-in-the-throat sonority that
was an intimation of some emotion that only *you* were in on.
"It's Judy."
"Judy," I exclaimed thoughtfully. I did have to think for a second;
after all it would have been what? more than twenty years? I don't
remember the sequence, but some place along that troubling time, I
had, not wanting to get them involved and not wanting them to be

in a "should I or shouldn't I" offer emotional support situation, I had,

passively and without resistance, ended it with, among others, our

very beloved friend Judy.

"I knew you weren't in Berkeley any more so I called your brother but . . ."

"I'm glad you did, very glad, but I asked him not to give my number, not to in general. So

how did you . . . ?"

"I didn't work in a law office for nothing, and I'm a law librarian now part-time but with

this tech stuff it may become no-time. I wouldn't mind being a stay-at-home mom for

my home boys, one mostly sweet 'old' man and a some-times sweet junior-high boy."

I hesitated as I thought 'isn't she a little . . . ?'

"He came with the deal, his dad's kid; that was ten years ago . . . where does the time go?"

"I've noticed."

"But how're you doing?"

"Oh, fair to middlin' . . . not too bad . . . considering."

"And Bel, do you ever . . . ?"

"I have no idea . . . no, never. She is, as kids do, growed up, that's all I know."

"You know, I've thought of her many times when Joey—he likes

'Joe,' but to me he's still Joey-Joe—was . . . she, in a way, she helped me be a mother, a

good mother."

"And you folks are doing good in . . . ?"

"Walnut Creek."

"Walnut Creek! One never knows, do one."

Chapter 31

*". . . dying nowadays is more gruesome, in many ways, namely more
lonely, mechanical and dehumanizing; at times it is even
difficult to determine technically when death occurred."*
Elizabeth Kubler-Ross

It's a kind of limbo. You're disqualified; you've fouled out on a bad
call. You're inhibited and constricted by legal and emotional strictures.
If, for instance, I'm having a sandwich in Union Square and an
amusingly cute kid comes by—with, certainly, a nanny or mommy
in tow—that would naturally elicit a smile, I don't smile. I'm a little
uneasy; who knows just who is subject to paranoia? The thing is, I
like kids, I appreciate kids, always have. I won't say I love kids in
general, but I have loved some kids, kith-and-kin kids. What would
my adversaries have made of such revealing statements?

On the other end of the spectrum, when, as happens in the Tenderloin,
I'm bothered by some aggressive pan-handler or nut-case, I just walk
away; I can't chance a cop-call situation. Then there are the prostitutes.

Some are very attractive, some are cops. I just say "no thank you, honey" and walk away. Any more, any conversation, as one guy at the Hubert found, is "solicitation." Just one slip-up and I'd be liable for a California Second Strike.

The damn pain and has me going all weak and wobbly. It's one more thing that is impossible to explain. After hearing variations of, "Oh, ya, I get so tired too," I don't even try to explain any more. It puts one in that limbo; while enervated to the edge of damnation you're sentenced to an exile of sorts.

I'd given away my chess clock. Time seemed to both drag and collapse exponentially. My graphite racket was back there with my 33-inch Joe DiMaggio Louisville Slugger of another, quite different time; a transformative and promising phase when venial errors tended to be forgiven.

.

But there was another kind of pain—a punishment—that I hadn't known anything about. Not that I'd anticipated any of this ordeal. When I was sentenced I thought everything was on the table: the conditions were set. Not so. I had completed all my obligations and then when Bel turned eighteen, I sent a letter to the court making it clear that I would cease paying support unless I was ordered to pay adult-support. I wouldn't, certainly not now, not after . . . after what? make my somewhat-less-beloved daughter the promises that parents tend to make.

I only had that rest-of-your life registration duty. But now, after all that went before, came the punishment phase—the undisclosed

sentence. It seems that registration is a license of sorts: the police
have license to harass you. One, two, three and one time four, they
come knocking at your door. Are you suspected of anything? hell,
no. Is there anything suspicious about your registration? hell, no.
Do those visits constitute an unreasonable search? I'd guess that's
the case. Is this policy a make-work program for the supposedly
understaffed SFPD? who knows? Are those cops just looking for
trouble? Who knows what's going on in the political aspects of
such cop-duty?

Then the Federal "Megan's Law" is passed and you're on the internet,
you're in virtual stocks. Is that retroactive sentencing? sure as hell it
is. Is that *ex post facto* law? hell, yes. Is that constitutional? well, it
passed the House 418 to zero. Now the state legislature is trying to
outdo the feds with "Jessica's Law," which will require every
registered sex-offenders to wear a GPS ankle bracelet and not live
within 200 yards of a park or school. You can imagine the hysterical
process that makes for such an impossible logistical problem. It
would seem that the lust for retribution makes it easy—perhaps
necessary—for fear-mongering politicians to promise—with little
girl's names—supposed security.

I don't know if it was a coincidence or not, but back when cable news
was reporting, *ad nauseam,* some grotesque murder of a child in
Florida or where ever, I'd get a loud-knocking visit. Then a woman
two doors down evidently combined my photo, address and
history from the internet and enlisted her little boy to rid the
neighborhood of such an obvious predator. In that instance—
luckily—the "victim" didn't substantiate to the any degree the

mother's fears—or hopes. But how long before some child gets
with the program and tells—once again—what mom or dad or
the cops may want to hear?

*(I know, I know, I shouldn't have thrown the kid's ball back to him.
I shouldn't have said "nice catch." I shouldn't have smiled.)*

I happened to notice the car pull up across the street. A non-descript
four-door, but you could tell; especially when a similar car, similarly
manned, slid in behind the first and parked about six feet from the curb.
They knock, hard.
"Who's there?" I ask.
No answer, no 'it's the police.' Just more knocking. I guess they don't
want the would-be host getting his gun. I go to the fridge and get a
bottle of beer. More knocking. "Hey, who's there?" They'll get in, one
way or another, five of the city's finest didn't come here to go away
with nothing.

"Police, we want to talk to you."
"OK," I say very loudly, "you woke me up, gimme a minute."
More hard knocking.
I get my bath towels, put them on the coffee table and take a drink of
beer.
The phone rings, who could that be? "Hello."
"Jeffrey Hodges, Sergeant Gerhardt, SFPD, I want you to open up, now."
"You have a warrant?"
"We have a warrant. Let us in or we're coming in."
"OK, sure, lemme get some clothes on."

I hang up and empty a vial of Valium into my left hand: a good hundred or so of saved-up 5 mg tablets. I wash down a multiple multiple dose with the Henry's for a chaser. I peel the Rx label and set it afire. Then I fan out my address book—it was, I remember, a gift from Rita—and light that: part of my life is ashes in a tea cup. Among various pens, hi-lighters and a letter opener in a glass cylinder on the coffee table, is an X-acto knife. The back-up: a cutting tool to make sure I don't get caught in an awkward half-alive situation. I rest my left foot on the towels—I don't want to make a big mess—and feel for the pulse behind the ankle bone. The first cut is tentative and doesn't do the job. I have to do this before I get too woozy; this isn't the time for experimental surgery. I just do it the old-fashioned way and cut across the prominent vein in my left wrist; that starts a bright letting . . . . I sit back and hang my bleeding arm over a plastic storage bin and wash down the remaining bitter pills with the soothing beer. I watch wisps of fog blowing roof-top high under— what else?—a low sky of dark clouds.

My room, my very homey and comfortable room seems somehow different. I look around at the birds on the wall—a red-wing black-bird, a sandpiper, an elegant egret, an . . . . All in their frames, unmoved by the scene they over-look; they will stay.

The cops will get in; by that time I will have checked out.